I E L L E

A REALM OF JANOS NOVEL
BY ANDRE SANTHOMAS

Ielle
by André SanThomas

2012 RoJ Publishing Paperback Edition

All rights reserved.

Dedication

To my husband, who is ever and always in my corner.
All my love, always.

Acknowledgements

Special thanks to the Erotica Readers and Writers Association, in particular Crissi, Shar and Lisabet. And to Chris for all his inspiration and assistance.

CHAPTER ONE
~ IELLE ~

"It's time."

Ielle took a deep breath and rose gracefully from the furs. She was nervous. Like all the girls of age on her world, she had years of training to prepare for this day. Still, she felt her stomach flutter now that it was time to carry out the fulfillment.

She stood, naked, her chest moving rapidly up and down until she calmed herself. She brought both hands up from her sides, stretched out as far as they could reach, palms up and open, arcing them until they met over her head. She brought her hands down, clasping her fingers tightly together and set-tling her arms under the full swell of both breasts. The soft weight of them rested on her forearms, the nipples peeking out, dusty pink. Yes, she was as ready as she could get.

The warm breeze brushed her skin. She had practiced the positions while naked of course, but she had never been in front of anyone but her teacher and the other girls unclothed. Unowned girls were kept carefully covered until this moment. Another breath. It was time.

She crossed the compound, hundreds of eyes turned toward her. Her bare feet picked up a light blue coating of dust from the ground as she walked. It was early yet, not too hot, but not too cold for her bare skin either. Men and women alike gazed at her, some even jostling for a better view. They were examining, weighing, evaluating as she moved toward the dais.

They all judged her worth, but only one judgment mattered. Some were dressed in the finery of the upper class, some in the ragged cloth of the poor. Everyone else was dressed in something, even if it might be skimpy or ragged.

She was naked and fully exposed, ready to be scored. She squeezed her fingers together a little tighter, knowing that there was more to come soon, hoping she would hold up well.

She had her first look at him when she crossed the small wooden bridge that spanned the light orange waters of the creek. He was tall, a few years older than she was. His eyes were dark, a deep brown that bored into her, even at a distance. He did not look nervous, not at all, but surely he must be. She breathed in and out slowly again. She would appear as collected as he did. She could feign confidence if he could.

Two men stood with him, one quite similar but bigger and broader, perhaps a brother or cousin. The other shorter, light haired, younger. His men, at his side for the ceremony. They would not know how her stomach fluttered more and more with every step closer to her destiny.

It seemed both an eternity and an instant then Ielle was before him. She was close enough to touch him, close enough for him to touch her. His face was strong, sure. There was something else.

A smirk. He was amused by her. She narrowed her eyes and shifted her calm countenance to something closer to a glare. She pulled herself back from outright defiance, but she did allow her face to let him know she was not strictly entertainment. Once the contract was fulfilled, she would be his property, yes. But she was not without value and substance herself.

The Oblate nodded and Ielle released her fingers, dropping her hands to her sides. The scribe made a note in the tablet. Her handmaidens stepped up, taking her hands straight out to the sides and holding her firmly, their fingers supporting the weight of her arms so that she should not tire during the judging. They did not hold her to keep her from fleeing. There were girls that struggled sometimes, often with dire results, but Ielle would not be one of them. There was no fear of that from those that knew her.

The Oblate spoke, his voice ringing out loudly, the crowd hushed and listening.

"Who judges the offering?"

"Kyr of Janos." He spoke with no hesitation, watching her as he answered. Perhaps he did not feign confidence after all. It seemed to be something he wore quite comfortably.

"Who stands with the judge?"

"Bylar of Janos." The bigger man spoke and the scribe recorded the information.

His eyes twinkled as he watched her display herself. She puzzled that her glare did not set him back at all. In fact, she realized that it only amused him more. He stepped forward, close in front of her. The examination would begin now.

She steeled herself, knowing from her training what steps were involved, knowing in a logical way what he would do. This was no longer hypothetical instruction from her teacher. This was the judging for the fulfillment of the contract. The weight of that knowledge sat on her heart but she took another breath to keep herself calm.

He brushed his fingers lightly over her face, both hands touching her skin for the first time, warm, strong, knowing. She held still, watching him intently, determined not to flinch or succumb. He trailed the tips across her forehead, her eyes closing as he stroked over the lids, then fluttering open again when they moved to her cheeks. He used only one finger to draw ever so lightly across her lower lip. The barest touch on her, tingling, tickling. She wanted to bite her lip, scratch it with her teeth, soothe the itch he was creating. She wanted to press her mouth into his touch, but she would not.

She held still, her breath gently blowing while he continued, watching her intently, cataloging her responses. She could tell he saw her battle, but she would not confirm it for him. She held still, like a statue under the hands of a sculptor, a living work of art.

He stroked her upper lip, the same tickle and itch that she was unable to scratch. She stared him down. He moved his finger from her mouth, touching her ears, a firm pinch on each lobe, but still she refused to flinch. He grinned, no longer making any pretense of hiding his mirth. He stroked his hands down her throat, trailing over her collar bones, her skin breaking out in goose bumps at the touch. She sucked in air and found herself inhaling his scent. Something spicy and warm, masculine and primal.

He hefted both breasts, cupping them from underneath, weighing them, eyes locked on hers. They filled his hands nicely, she was neither too small nor too large. He nodded at the Oblate and the scribe made a note on a tablet.

He took her nipples between his thumbs and index fingers. He pressed and released several times until they started to pebble. She took slow, calming breaths, remembering her training, willing herself not to flush under his scrutiny. She couldn't prevent the gasp when he pinched hard, then twisted. She couldn't hide how they tightened under his touch. He could not know how her core clenched. A feeling she had never had before. Another nod to the scribe, another note.

He moved behind her, fingers combing through her long dark hair, following it from the crown of her head to the small of her back. He gathered it and draped it over her shoulder. She sucked in again, her hair brushed over her sensitized skin and teased her hardened nipple. He was tracing his fingers over her smooth back, following the curve of her shoulder blades, feeling each bone in her spine. He cupped her rear cheeks, clenching and releasing, squeezing her flesh. She wanted to close her eyes, escape from the process but she would not.

His hands were on her thighs, tracking downwards, flexing into her skin, tracing the muscles down the back of her legs, even stopping a moment to tickle behind her knees. He was in front of her again, working his way up over calves and thighs, kneeling in front of her to be able to reach, his breath close against her. She took another calming breath, knowing he was soon to do the final tests.

He rested his hands on her legs, looking her over a moment before he tugged on the small patch of curls that her handmaidens had left during the denuding. She clamped down on her lip, determined not to cry out while he pulled. Blessedly, he released her before many hairs pulled free. He looked up at her, watching her when he dipped his finger into the crease between her lower lips. She held his gaze.

She knew he felt the moisture that was gathering there. She clenched her hands, waiting for the inevitable.

There it was. He slipped his finger into her and she fought against the grimace she would otherwise make. Although they discussed this in the training, the actual insertion was saved for this moment. If he refused her, she would still be intact for another judging, but her value would drop. If she should be refused enough times, she would be consigned to the auctions, ending up as a house girl at best, the rentals at worst. She pushed that ugly thought from her head and concentrated on the here and now instead.

He smiled broadly when he pulled his finger from her, wiping the evidence of her arousal across the front of her thigh. There was a positive murmur from those in the crowd that were close enough to see, the word spreading in waves to those at the rear. He nodded again to the scribe, then stepped away to consult with Bylar.

She lowered her arms. Once again she clasped her fingers together and tucked her arms under her breasts while she waited. She couldn't hear what he said, but she could see the animated discussion going on in quiet voices, the occasional laugh, the looks and nods in her direction. Was he really requiring so much thought? Was he just torturing her? Might he actually be considering a refusal? She was getting a bit light-headed and reminded herself to breathe, surprised that these final moments were proving to be the most stressful of the process. She had hundreds of hours of practice and schooling to prepare for the ritual but there was little talk of this part of the process.

He turned to the Oblate and she held her breath. It would be a crushing blow if he should refuse her. Until now it really had not occurred to her that might be possible.

"Do you accept the offering, Kyr of Janos?"

"Yes, Kyr of Janos accepts the offering, Ielle of Harku."

CHAPTER TWO
~ KYR ~

Kyr settled himself into the furs on the dais. His men sat cross-legged near him to watch. The handmaidens retreated, their job done for the day. The Oblate and scribe stepped back to the distant corner, able to see and record the fulfillment of the contract, yet out of the way. Ielle stepped forward and waited for the drum beat to begin.

Now she would dance for him. Kyr considered her as she prepared to begin the next phase of the ceremony. She had that beautiful long dark hair, nearly to her waist. It was soft and silky when he ran his hands through it. Her skin was pale and creamy with deep blue eyes like the mountains of their homeland. Her lips were soft and dusty pink, her nipples were firm and responsive to his touch.

Her spark is what really caught his attention though. There were many girls that were beautiful. He preferred a girl that was smart, loyal, confident. If she was as beautiful as this one, so much the better.

He knew she was meant for him as soon as he saw her making her way to the dais. It hit his heart like a bolt from the sky. He had not known it would feel thus. He thought he might know when he saw her, might know during the judging, but he also thought he would need to consider and reflect. It was not so.

The judging only confirmed it. The way she held herself intrigued him. Nervous surely. Trying hard not to let anyone know it. Strong. She would match him. She submitted to him, but she retained her spirit. She was proud, but she did not hold herself above others.

The drummer stepped up, standing behind Kyr and his men. Ielle settled her hands on her naked hips, looking directly at Kyr. He watched her take a moment and then a smoldering look came to her eyes, seducing him, brimming with passion yet to be unleashed. He caught his breath but quickly contained himself. It would not do to let others know how she affected him already.

She pointed her foot, stretching it out languidly in front of her, bending her other knee, crouching low, raising her hands over her head, entwining the fingers and bowing before him. She pushed up on her left leg then drew her right leg back until she stood tall, bringing her hands down, running them seductively over the soft skin of breasts and torso. He clenched his fingers remembering their feel. She moved exactly with the sound of the drum when she rose on tip toe and twirled before him, one complete circle causing her long, dark hair to spin out around her.

She stopped, staring him down, challenging him. Her look was pure lust even though he knew she could have no real idea yet of what that might feel like. She stepped closer to him, dropping to one knee and extending the other leg, hovering with her foot nearly touching him. He could feel the warmth of her, even though they did not connect.

She bent over, caressing her hands from her toes up her calf and over her thigh, skimming past her stomach as she arched her back away from him. She whipped herself forward, bending double again before rising to her feet and taking a step to spin away from him.

The sound of the drum followed her movements, building in intensity, mirroring his own heart beat. Ielle stood before him, circling her hands gracefully in front of her body. She sank slowly to her knees, legs not quite closed, a glimpse of her lower lips teasing him. His blood pumped hard and he reminded himself to exercise restraint.

She reached her hand out then trailed it into his hair, caressing his temple before abruptly pulling back. By the gods, her touch was magical. It brought a punch of heat straight to his groin.

She rested both hands on the dais and pushed herself to her toes, rear end high in the air, head down, hair trailing. She undulated as she straightened.

He watched her breasts and the way they bounced and shuddered. He could not wait to taste them, lick his tongue over them, press them and tease them until she was insane under him. Once again she twirled, but this time moved the extra half turn to display her rear. She bent to touch her toes.

He was breathing hard. He could see her lower lips peeking at him, the slight glistening already beginning to coat them. He pictured thrusting himself into her and shifted a bit on the furs to find a more comfortable position when his cock stirred in response. She rose and completed the spin, her hair cascading out around her. What would it be like to have that silky mass trailing over his bare skin as she rode him?

She dropped down to hands and knees, crawling slowly towards him. She arched her back bringing her rear up. She kept her eyes on his, measuring the look in them, noting his interest. Bylar was shifting uncomfortably, adjusting himself too and grinning at Kyr. Bylar knew him well.

She reached out to Kyr and ran her hand over his knee, gently circling her fingers over the cloth, trailing them up his thigh, teasing, tempting, not touching that sacred spot, but promising so much more later. He watched her fingers move, tensing his muscles so as not to give in to her yet. She brushed over his stomach then pulled away.

The drumbeat was louder now following her heat, echoing in his head. Back on her feet, she slowed, taking several beats to complete a turn while her hands stroked her breasts and belly, hips and thighs. He was breathing hard and she was covered in a sheen of sweat. Her own chest was pumping, drawing in air as she moved and teased.

She came right up to him, turning away and sinking to her hands and knees, arching her back and gyrating her ass ever so close to him. He would enjoy taking her in this position, slapping her smooth pale cheeks while he pumped into her. She dropped flat on her belly, spreading her arms and legs wide, rocking her hips against the flooring.

She rolled to her back and spread her arms and legs wide again. He smiled to himself. He would enjoy taking her in that position too. She pillowed her hands under her head before pulling her feet back until her knees bent and her lower lips spread fully open. She shifted her hips up and down, closing her eyes, rolling her head back and forth as though she was in the throes of passion. Yes, he would have her thus, screaming and begging.

The drummer beat harder and faster, growing, climbing. He could see her heat rising, radiating from her, enveloping him. He could smell her, feel her need and desire. She sat up again, cupping her breasts, offering them, her legs spread open wide, toes pointed gracefully, displayed for him. On the final beat of the drum she dropped her head submissively, giving herself to him. Her chest was heaving as she caught her breath, her skin was flushed and shining.

It was his turn again. The thin delicate notes of the flute began to waft over the assemblage. Ielle held her position.

She left her head down, but peeked up to meet his gaze while he rose and stepped towards her. She was so fixated on him she gasped when she was lifted from behind.

Bylar had her on her feet, but she still cupped her breasts offering them to him, her head still bowed. Good girl. She had been well trained and exercised self-discipline.

Kyr moved quickly and hefted her over his shoulder, his hand resting on her rear, fondling her. The crowd cheered as he turned to them. She hung passively over his back, her hair brushing the floor. He enjoyed the feel of her, absorbing her weight easily.

He deposited her on the raised altar, laying her back, using his hands to spread her thighs open before him. Bylar took a place behind her, bracing head and shoulders up so that she could not help but watch Kyr. It was part of the fulfillment that she see him, to know who would take her, own her. It had been done this way since the early times, the mandate of the gods. His best friend and cousin would ensure it occurred. Bylar held her hands, she was not to touch, just to feel and absorb and submit.

Kyr bent between her thighs and inhaled her scent. She smelled of flowers and sunshine and heat and passion. He enjoyed how she twitched when he took his tongue and licked it across the skin just below her navel. The tongue teased her skin, circling her navel, his fingers kneading, warming into her thighs. He brushed his lips over the crease where her leg joined her torso, tasting the salt.

He brought goose bumps to her flesh. He grinned when he saw them, teasing her. He reached for her breasts, palming them, rubbing his thumbs over the tips until they were tight and puckered. He nodded to his man, Makir and soon two small inverted cups appeared. Makir heated them with a candle then settled them over her nipples. The suction would pull at them, keeping them erect. A slight moan slipped from her lips, faint, yet he was sure he heard it. Her eyes were the darkest shade of blue ever. She watched him while he stroked a thick roughened finger along her damp slit and he felt her quiver in response. He brought his hand to her lips, transferring the moisture to them. She tipped her tongue over her mouth, soothing the tickle and tasting herself in the process, just as he intended.

He took her mouth with his, possessing it, forcing her lips apart, thrusting his tongue inside. She gasped, sucking him in. She was panting when he pulled back. She could not contain her groan when he entered her with his finger, sliding in and out of her wet channel. She rocked her hips against the hard altar, trying to get closer to him.

He captured her mouth again, pulling the air from her lungs as he ravaged her mouth. He plunged himself into her with no warning, swallowed her wail, giving her time to adjust to the feel of him. She tightened her muscles around him, his hardness filling her completely. She would know now, this was her purpose. She was made for him, tight, hot, wet, wanting.

He had not disrobed, that would be unseemly for a man during the public ceremony. His hard cock and balls discretely slipped through a slit in the fabric so that he might take her in public as the contract demanded. His pants rubbed roughly on the tender skin of her inner thighs. She would be sore later but she would learn to cherish the reminder of his possession.

The cups tugged at her nipples, keeping them sensitive and needy. He felt the change when she relaxed into the sensations. She would call on her training and remember her role, accept the feelings instead of fighting them. Good girl.

When he started moving again, she did more than submit. She met his thrusts, matching him, needing him, rising higher and higher. He nipped at her bottom lip, making her moan and writhe. Bylar held her hands securely and he could see her fingers twitching, grasping at air instead of his arms or hair. He forgot about the crowd, his men, the Oblate, the scribe and gave himself over to the sensations of the moment. He pulled the suction cups from her breasts, releasing the pressure, then replacing it with his mouth, rubbing his teeth over the tip. She thrashed her head from side to side, arching her back, pressing her nipple further into his mouth. He alternated between the two nipples, tormenting them, making her crazy with need.

He sucked harder at her, ramming his cock into her, fast and strong, slamming the breath out of her in little gusts. He slipped a finger between them, stroking her quickly, flicking the hardened woman's nub until she trembled.

She was screaming, clenching him, milking him as he shot his hot fluid into her. He thrust a few more times and he thought he heard cheering, but could not focus on it.

He was back on her mouth, gentler now but still in charge, stroking her lips with his tongue, soothing the bruise from his bites. He pushed himself up, smiling, then slipped himself from her. Makir handed him a cloth and he quickly wiped the fluids and blood before tucking himself back into his clothing.

She slumped on the altar as though she would never want to move again. Kyr caught his breath, watching her. Bylar let go of her hands and shifted back from her, gently lowering her head to the stone. She closed her eyes, panting and glowing with left over sensations. She was shining with sweat, little tendrils of her hair damp on her brow, a sheen between her breasts.

Kyr took her hands and pulled her up to a sitting position. The ceremony was nearly over. She must witness the final stage.

The Oblate stepped up, taking the cloth from Kyr. He inspected it, speaking quietly to the scribe. The Oblate held the cloth aloft and announced, "The contract is fulfilled."

The crowd cheered and applauded, Bylar and Makir clapped Kyr on the back. "Let this female forever be known as Ielle-kyr of Janos, property of the first order."

He felt a kick to his gut at the words. She was his now. Owned property. He knew he was ready for such a responsibility, but the weight of it struck him unexpectedly. He must take care not to let her down as her owner. He already carried the weight as Hausa of Janos and was used to heavy burdens, but this was somehow even more personal. He hoped he could live up the example his late father set, both as a Hausa and an owner.

Kyr smiled at her and reached for a small sack. From it he took a bright metal chain. The links were smooth and rounded when he worked it through his fingers. He watched her breath quicken and moved it to make sure it caught the light.

He wrapped it around her waist, resting it on her hips before securing it into a small lock with his crest on it. The chain fit perfectly, he could slip his finger between it and her skin. It was a visible sign that she was owned and by whom. A reminder to her that she was his. She would not be able to remove it herself. It would remain on her forever as the sign that she was Ielle-kyr of Janos.

CHAPTER THREE
~ IELLE ~

Bylar rested his hands on her shoulders while Kyr tied
her hands behind her back. She stood waiting while
the men spoke and payment was made to the Oblate
and the scribe. His light haired man stood near her,
keeping an eye that she did not flee. Some girls tried
to run, but it was always a futile effort. No one in the
crowd would grant them sanctuary. The ceremony
was always held away from both their homes, there
would be no allegiance to either of them.

Ielle suspected some girls ran to excite their owner. Perhaps some men enjoyed the pretense. Some ran
from fear, or immaturity, a result of poor training. Or
poor character. To run would be foolhardy as well as
disgraceful. Should the new owner not find the game

amusing, there would be a discard. The girl would receive a severe punishment from the Oblate, then be sent to the rentals.

Ielle had no thoughts to flee. Aside from her up-bringing, the lingering thrill of his touch was still on her, the awakening of her sex, the freedom of her lust. She did not know if another could have done the same, but she thought it unlikely. This Kyr of Janos was meant for her. She had no such thoughts for any other man standing on the dais or milling in the crowd.

She was aware of his every move. She could surely pick him blindfolded from the entire crowd just by his scent. Being near him was intoxicating. Ielle said a quiet prayer of thanks to the gods for her good fortune so far. It seemed The Council had cho-sen well for her.

No one knew exactly how the Council made their choices. They received divine inspiration direct-ly from the gods. It was not the place of the owners or the property to question it. Instead, when girls were of age and their training complete, at some point there would be a calling from the Council. Some girls were called up quickly, some waited for a very long time. It was the will of the gods.

The men must petition for their property. It was not something to be done lightly. They must be ma-ture enough to take on the responsibility and the

Council must agree. Then they too waited until the Council had an offering for them. The men confirmed the match at the judging or they tried again with another.

The conversation among the men was done, it was time to leave. Most times the women were given a cloak or shift to wear. She frowned realizing that Kyr did not seem inclined to do so. It was within his rights to do with her as he wished. Should he wish to keep her naked and bound forever, he might do so, but most men did not. She was quickly realizing that he was not as most men.

She trailed along behind them, Bylar holding her where her hands joined. It was a light touch, but he completely controlled her with only a finger. She felt his dominion over her, yet it was different than the feeling she had with Kyr. With Kyr she was owned. Something much more personal and intense she could not explain.

There was discussion when they reached the mounts. The mareshi were difficult animals, requiring years of training to fully control. They were grand beasts, tall and furry, able to carry men and their supplies for long distances.

If they cooperated, they would quickly cover much ground. If they did not a rider could easily be trampled in an instant. Kyr bounced lightly onto the mount, comfortable in his seat. Bylar hefted her and dumped her across the saddle, stomach down in front of Kyr. She bit her lip and did not protest but could not prevent the oof that fell from her when her belly landed hard.

Bylar quickly and crudely braided her hair into a long plait then secured it with a small piece of twine looped to the top of the saddle. The mareshi was too tall for her hair to drag upon the ground, but this would ensure that it would not distract the animal or tangle in a hoof. It did not pull her hair, but it was one more restraint and she felt it as such. Kyr patted her ass and dipped a finger between her still damp thighs. By the gods, he was stroking her in a way that made her heat rise again. Would she ever get enough of his touch on her?

He chuckled when she squirmed under his touch. She pressed her hips into his hand, into the saddle, wanting more.

He brought his hand down sharply on her skin several times, the sound reverberating in her ears. The sting reached her brain a moment later causing her to gasp quietly.

"Keep still, Ielle-kyr. We don't want you falling off and being trampled to death on your first day." Damn him. He was laughing at her again. She could hear it in his voice. His men were laughing loudly too, enjoying the show. She was glad he couldn't see her face, flushed red with anger, shame, desire. She wished she could be as a child and stamp her feet, but those days were gone ages ago. Thankfully, he decided it was time to move on.

The mareshi bolted forward. It was uncomfortable and disconcerting to be thrown over his mount like a sack of grain, but after a few minutes she became accustomed to the rhythm of the beast and was able to find it bearable. Again her training came to her ears. Resistance brought tension, tension brought discord. Relax, submit, absorb, embrace, find harmony. In this case, hardly harmony, but at least a reduction in misery.

It seemed hours before the mareshi slowed and came to a halt. The brilliant sun was low on the horizon. Another smack landed on her rump.

"We will make camp tonight, Ielle-kyr. We are still some distance from your new home." Kyr himself unhooked her hair and pulled her from the mareshi, holding her closely against him while she found her footing. Her stomach ached from pressing into the saddle, her hands and feet tingled from the unnatural position. Still, she reveled in his embrace, even if it was more clinical concern for his expensive investment than interest in her personal comfort. She found herself leaning heavily into him, drawing from his warmth. He stroked his hands over her back, feeling her silky skin. The binding at her wrists was suddenly loosened and he took her hands into his, rubbing them gently until the sting-ing went away.

"I should inspect you for damages," he said with a chuckle. Damn him! Would he never cease to find her so amusing?

"I'm quite fine now, thank you." She pulled her-self together and straightened her spine, even though her sore ribs protested the movement. "Shall I pre-pare the meal?"

He laughed loudly and heartily. "She has dis-missed us boys, do you see? Or perhaps it is not all of us that she has dismissed, just her master, eh? Yes, make the meal. Makir has the provisions." She turned to walk away, determined to keep her pride intact no matter how much he baited her.

"Ielle-kyr," he called, reaching out to grab her arm before she could move too far away. He pulled her tightly against him, reminding her of his hard strength and how it fit her softness so well. "Enjoy your dignity now. Tonight I will have you writhing, pleading, desperate for me. More so than the fulfill-ment. Remember that."

He was infuriating! Rotten pithtai worm snake! She glared at the spot where he held her arm, disdain radiating from her until finally he let her go. She used all her will not to smack the smirk off his face. She turned away, planning to take out her frustration on the fire Bylar was stacking for her.

She banged around and slammed pieces of the kindling and lids of the pots with far more force than necessary. She noticed that all three men wisely decided to keep a bit of distance from her while she did so, settling themselves beside the bower they had constructed. They lounged on the furs telling jokes and teasing each other while she worked. She thought she was finally putting her annoyance in check, but she couldn't help but replay his words. The fulfillment was beyond description. He was promising more, daring her to more, threatening her with more. Could it be possible?

Though she worked quickly, it was dark when the meal was ready. She ladled the food into a bowl, adding a hot hunk of bread, then took several deep breaths to prepare herself. No matter what she was feeling, she would show her proper training. She carefully wiped the bowl of any drips then carried it to him, sinking to her knees at his feet. Her legs parted, her sex visible to him. The air was cooling now, the camp lit by the soft glow of the fire pit.

Using two hands, she slid the warm bowl over her thigh, across her mound then back the other direction tracing the chain hanging low on her stomach. She circled the bowl upwards, brushing her breasts, lingering a moment over her heart before gently kissing the rim. Ielle bowed her head and offered it towards him. "Your meal is prepared and humbly offered to you. May it bring you health, wisdom and happiness."

He left her waiting a moment, her hands outstretched holding his bowl, her back arched to display her breasts, her gaze cast downwards as required.

The warmth of the bowl seeped into her palms as she waited for him to take the offering. It seemed an eternity before he slipped it from her fingers, finally allowing her to drop her hands to her thighs and raise her head to watch him sup. He deliberately turned the bowl to the place where she kissed it, trailing his tongue across the lingering moisture then blatantly licking his lips. He winked at her, causing her to flush scarlet at the thought of him licking her skin later that evening.

He sipped at the broth, nodding thoughtfully, using his fingers to pull a hearty piece of meat from the stew. She watched him chew, far more interested than she wanted to admit in his reaction to her cooking skills. He swallowed and nodded. "You may serve, Ielle-kyr." She smiled before she realized it, lighting up at his approval.

Quickly she returned to the fire then one after the other brought a bowl to Bylar and Makir. She knelt before each of them in turn, careful to keep her knees tightly together. She brought the bowl straight to her forehead touching it there then bowing with the words "Kyr of Janos offers you this meal. May it nourish your body and brotherhood." When she finished, she returned to Kyr's feet, kneeling once again before him.

He smiled at her, genuine and warm this time instead of teasing. "At the risk of swelling your head and encouraging your vanity, this is excellent food. I did not know that tinned kafai could be so tender and tasty. And I have never had such fine bread. You've done well and I am pleased." He held a piece of the stew meat towards her, forcing her to lean in to take it with her mouth. His fingers lingered a moment, teasing her lips before releasing the food.

She fed from him, realizing as she did she was actually quite hungry. She had not eaten since hours before the ceremony, but so much had gone on this long day she had not noticed.

The food warmed her, nutrients coursing again through her veins. She was quick to refill the bowls for the men, especially Kyr's since she felt guilty at how much of it she consumed herself. He did not seem to mind, continuing to feed her at his feet, giving her two or three bites for every one he took himself.

She finally shook her head when he brought a piece of the dinner her way. He raised an eyebrow at her. "You'll need your energy tonight, take this last bit of bread." She blushed again and Bylar and Makir grinned like youngsters. She did, however, take the final bite from him.

"Good girl. I'd have you do the washing up, but I know this has been a long day and I want to make the best use of the energy you have left. Makir has kindly offered to take care of the kitchen and Bylar has kindly offered to escort you to the waterway to bathe before you join me in my furs."

"Thank you," she said, rising to her feet. Bylar was immediately by her side, walking down the dark path, lighting the way with a torch. They soon arrived at the shimmering shore of the waterway. The clear orange water danced in the moonlight, gentle and shallow with a sandy beach.

Nearby a waterfall danced, showering drops into the stream. Ielle entered the water gratefully, happy to have the chance to bathe the sweat and the sex, the dust and the dirt of the day from her pale skin. She was pleased that the water still retained the heat of the day and settled comfortably on her skin.

"Ielle! Catch!" She turned just in time to grab a flying bit of soap from Bylar. He followed it with a washcloth and she smiled sweetly at him before she turned her back and set to work scrubbing. She ducked under the waterfall rinsing, water sluicing off her moonlit skin.

She stood still on the beach, combing her fingers through her hair, carefully braiding it across five strands, much prettier than Bylar had done for her earlier. None the less, his attempt had been thoughtful. Or at least practical. Her variation was also decorative.

They started back to the camp. She chilled with the dampness on her skin. Bylar noted her shiver and stopped in the path, shrugging off his shirt and draping it over her shoulders. It fell to her knees and simple as it was, it brought tears to her eyes. She had been completely naked for hours and hours, looked upon and stared at by hundreds. Now this one piece of cloth not only served to warm her, but shield her as well.

"Thank you." She was hardly able to speak. She used her fingers to dash the tears away, embarrassed that she let her emotions overcome her. This was hard, harder than she thought it would be. She had been shielded and kept from men, tucked away in training and robes. Now they were all pulled away at once and she was naked in every way.

She knew this was how it might be. She spent the day ignoring it, now it could not be denied. This was to be her reality. She blinked rapidly, breathing deeply, working to push back the tears before she went on.

Bylar waited patiently for her to be ready. He did not seem surprised or embarrassed by her outburst. He smiled softly at her. "My first charge is and always will be Kyr, but you are my second charge,

Ielle. As long as you remain important to Kyr, you remain important to me as well."

She nodded, silently continuing along the path, overwhelmed with the events of the day, unable to process what might happen next. Just before they arrived at the camp, Bylar stopped again, retrieving his damp shirt from her and slinging it casually over his shoulder. She pulled herself out of her introspection long enough to notice that he was strong and well muscled with a blood red body marking running across his right shoulder and down to his elbow. It was intricate and dramatic. Body marks were not unheard of, but they were not especially common. She had only seen a few and nothing that was done so beautifully.

He grinned at her gaze. "Kyr and I had them done together when we were quite young. Really not old enough, but Kyr was stubborn and I was reckless. At least we had the good sense to have an expert artist do the work. I suspect you will see Kyr's in just a few minutes. And a whole lot more, I'd wager." She could not help but blush again.

CHAPTER FOUR
~ KYR ~

Kyr was under the bower waiting for her. Makir had packed away the kitchen supplies and made pallets for himself and Bylar on the other side of the mareshi so they would have a pretense of privacy. He caught a glimpse of Bylar's head over the brush and could see he was talking to her. Kyr smiled and shook his head. Probably telling her embarrassing stories about him if he knew Bylar at all.

She stepped clear of the brush and crossed to him. He watched her move, delighted with her. The firelight reflected on her pale skin, giving her a glow in the darkness.

She was beautiful, full of fire and spark, maintaining an impressive dignity despite the battles that waged within her. Most importantly she was full of passion. He would earn her complete devotion soon enough, he could feel it growing already.

She slipped gracefully to her knees before him, cupping her breasts and offering them to him. His own desire pushed up a notch. Her years of training showed well in her movements and control. He enjoyed that about her, but it would be his mission tonight to break past that reserve and have her completely abandon all propriety with him. He watched her nipples gently move up and down with her breathing. The chill of the bathing had perked them already. He closed his eyes a moment, remembering how they tasted earlier.

"Bartu," he said, sitting back and waiting for her to move. He watched her suck her breath in, her chest rising with the effort. She moved immediately as he expected she would. She crawled sensuously towards him, his eyes following the sway of her raised ass. When she was within a breath of him, she turned, lowering herself to her elbows, knees wide apart, her back end displayed for him, his for the taking.

He rubbed his hands over the rounded ass, feeling her tense briefly before she relaxed. Excellent. He increased the pressure from stroking to kneading, watching his fingers press into her flesh. He took his thumbs and spread her cheeks apart, hearing her gasp and flinch. He grinned, teasing her again, running his fingers through the cleft, even circling the dark hole there, just to make her wonder how he might use her tonight.

He took a moment to play with the chain around her waist, running it through his fingers, pulling it so that it rubbed over her skin, circling her, reminding her that she was owned. More than owned really. Owned by Kyr of Janos. He laughed to himself, enjoying the way it hit her each time he made such a point to call her Ielle-kyr. Reinforcing for her that she was his.

He leaned forward and pressed his lips to the small of her back, licking his tongue out and tracing her skin. His hands returned to her rear, pressing and massaging. He carefully moved his fingers close to her lower lips, but did not touch, just enough to make her wonder when he would.

He slapped a hand against her flank, watching her jump then still. He slapped again, much harder this time, eliciting only a gasp even though the skin reddened with a sharp handprint that would probably linger a while. Good girl. He knew it hurt. By the gods, he was glad he didn't have to admit that last slap stung his own hand. But she did not scream and stamp her feet and whine.

It would be up to him to ensure he did not go too far. She would not be the one to do so. He felt a tenderness for her and the weight of the responsibility. That was their way, but he knew that many girls did not embrace it as fully. They could not or would not help themselves, flailing about, whining like children at the slightest provocation. That was not his Ielle.

Worse yet, many men allowed their girls to run them, disgraceful though that was. They fooled themselves into thinking they were still in charge. He was pleased she did not end up with one of those men. She would never be as satisfied as she would be with him. The Council had chosen extremely well for him and as it turned out, for her too.

He moved his hands to the back of her creamy thighs, first stroking them delicately, gentling her really. He loved mixing the soft and the hard. The sharp and the smooth. It played on a woman's senses in a special way. It filled them with anticipation, overloading their systems until a final push put them into ecstasy. He took his own calming breath imagining it.

He gave a hard pinch on the inside of her thigh, high up on the delicate skin, ever so close to her core. She jumped and yelped, her breathing quickening. More soothing massage, then a tighter, longer pinch even higher on the other side. This time she swallowed her squeal, making only a tiny whimper. He read the noise she made, not just pain he was sure, also desire. He leaned close and blew his breath along the crack of her ass, watching her shiver as the warmed moist air touched her skin.

He brought his hand up from underneath, surprising her by thrusting two fingers inside her core. He stroked his other hand over the small of her back, soothing, reassuring while he felt the texture of her inner walls. He was rewarded with a low husky moan. Yes. He was sure she was still sore from the way he pounded this very part of her just this morning, but she was built for this, built for him and she knew it.

He rotated his hand back and forth, then spread his fingers a bit, experimenting with her width. She was tight and actively clamping down on him. He stifled his own moan, imagining that sensation on his hard cock. Her thighs were quivering when he pulled his soaked hand from her. He lifted it to his face, smelling her scent. He considered a moment.

"Shaiku, Ielle-kyr."

She immediately rolled to her back, laying on the soft furs, using her hands to push her breasts up, pinching the nipples lightly between thumb and forefingers. The soles of her feet were pressed together and pulled up as far as possible, spreading her knees wide, completely exposing her sex. Her mouth parted, open for his use. He nudged her feet a bit higher, watching her wince and her muscles strain.

ANDRÉ SANTHOMAS

"Pinch those nipples as your master would do, Ielle-kyr. You represent his hand." She moaned but tightened her fingers as much as possible, her face betraying the pain for a moment until she settled into it. She was breathing hard, her skin flushed and shining with sweat. He smiled again, so pleased with her effort for him. Nothing half-hearted for his Ielle.

He leaned over her, bringing his still damp fingers below her nose. "Smell yourself, Ielle-kyr." He watched her breathe.

Her lungs must be full of her scent. She would know she could not hide how needy she was. "Taste yourself, Ielle-kyr." He brought the wet fingers to her mouth, slipping them inside her lips. She sucked at them greedily, stroking with her tongue, pulling every bit of her sticky fluid from them. He shuddered imagining that talented mouth working on him. Meanwhile she pinched and pressed and rubbed and rolled her nipples for him, pebbled and as hard now as any he had ever seen. Her juices glistened on her sex.

He took his hand from her mouth and returned it to her core. This time his thumb rested on her woman's nub, brushing it while he pumped his fingers back and forth, a parody of events to come. She twitched and began to writhe under him, exactly as he predicted earlier. She was moaning now, whimpering, involuntary little noises drifting from her. He smirked, recalling her scream at the ceremony. He would make her scream for him every time, if for no other reason than to tease her with it later.

He pulled out again, delighted at her groan. Yes, she had been close. He would make her wait, though it might kill them both. Once again he fed her, closing his eyes and taking deep breaths at the feel of her mouth on his skin. He took his hand away and replaced it with his mouth, moaning into her at the touch of her lips on his. He thrust his tongue into her, beating hers back, taking charge of her, sucking the air from her, tasting her sex still, owning her. She was pressing herself up to him, trying to meet him, submitting to him but certainly not passive.

No, not his Ielle. They were both panting when he pulled back and traced her lip with his tongue before nibbling it between his teeth. It was still swollen from his bites this morning. She would be more so tomorrow. He resolved to make an effort to ensure her lip was permanently full, a sign of her use.

He was uncomfortably hard. So close to just ravaging her. He sat back, leaving her squirming, her fingers still steadily working her nipples, her thighs still splayed. He pulled his shirt off, revealing his muscled chest. She stared at the blood red body mark covering his shoulder and running down his arm past the elbow towards the wrist. He remembered the day he received it, and the censure of his father

ANDRÉ SANTHOMAS

that evening. He grinned. It was worth it. He pushed thoughts of his father away and shucked his pants, tossing them casually aside.

He was naked, thick and ready. She was squirming and moaning before him. He felt the primal call of the ancestors, she was his. He pushed her feet apart, hooking her ankles over his shoulders, teasing his cock at her entrance. She was so slick, her hips were rocking, trying to find a way to draw him in.

He leaned over her, pushing her hand from a breast and replacing it with his mouth, keeping her working on the other one for him. Her head thrashed and he thought he heard a word as he stroked his teeth over her breast. One of his hands toyed with her chain, the other clamped into her thigh. He flicked the nipple with his tongue, soothing then sucking hard until her back arched off the furs in ecstasy and torment.

"Please..." Yes, he heard it that time, grinning around the mouthful of breast. He wiggled his hips, feeling the head brush her slick skin, but still not entering her. He could smell her arousal, taste her sweat.

They were locked in battle. She was a worthy opponent, but he would win. She would be pleading with all her might in a moment, he could hold out. He flicked her sex with a single hard stroke at the same time he clamped his lips hard onto her nipple.

She yelled, a tear slipping from her while she pushed her hips off the furs searching for his touch. "Please, please... I beg you to take me." She panted and arched. "Use your property please, Kyr of Janos, owner of Ielle-kyr."

He released her breast and answered her plea with his cock, holding himself still inside her while she tried to entice him to pump. Clenching and releasing against him. She was babbling, begging, he couldn't even focus on the exact words anymore, only their intent. She was as he promised, needy, desperate for him, ruined forever for anyone else. Perfect.

He slid slowly, slowly back, nearly out of her before he slammed into her, thrusting completely. Lubricated by her fluids, he slid in to the hilt even though he knew his girth filled her a bit more than was comfortable. No matter, she was responding to that conflict, it was firing her lust, freeing her from her internal restraints. Again and again he pumped, the only thought in his head to take her, possess her as no one else ever had or would.

When he was close to spilling he flicked her again, finally spurting his hot fluid into her, blessedly satiated. He was vaguely aware she was screaming, squeezing him impossibly hard inside her, her body shaking with spasms, her skin flushed, eyes closed.

He collapsed onto her, stroking her arm, pillowing his head on her breasts, resting his hard weight on her softness. Her heart beating strong and fast in his ear, he was sure his was the same. He became aware of the chill of the night air, reaching for a warm fur to cocoon them into.

She was tracing his body mark, fingers massaging over it, a tongue licking at the parts of it she could reach. The soft light of the fire flickered nearby, an island of light under the blanket of stars that peeked through the boughs over their heads.

"You were pleasing tonight, Ielle-kyr."

CHAPTER FIVE
~ IELLE ~

She slept in his furs and in his arms. He casually tossed his leg across her hip while they slept, his hand resting on the soft mound of her breast. She snuggled her bare rear into his groin, seeking his heat during the chilly night.

She woke to the unfamiliar weight of him. She started to stretch before she realized there wouldn't be much she could move until he shifted. Should she risk waking him? What ways might she tempt him into the day? She had not quite reached a decision when he squeezed her breast, his hand warm and strong on her skin.

She shifted to her back, smiling up at him. "Good dawn to you, Ielle-kyr," he said, returning her

ANDRÉ SANTHOMAS

smile before taking her mouth. She instantly trans-
formed from lingering sleep and languid afterglow
to burning desire for him. By the gods, did he possess some magic elixir? His scent, his touch, his taste,
all of it a drug she had no desire to resist.

It was some time later that they emerged from
the furs. It was still early, but well past the dawn.
Makir and Bylar had packed the provisions and readied the mareshi. There were only a few items left to
tend to so that they could leave and arrive home before nightfall. Once again, Bylar escorted her to the
waterway. She bathed quickly, the water cold, the
early morning air brisk when it touched her wet skin.

She wished she could soak in a warm pool and
massage her aching muscles. It seemed there was no
part of her, inside or out, that did not feel the results
of yesterday's activities. Some from the unceremoni-
ous position over the mareshi, the rest from the
heavenly pounding he had given her twice yesterday
and again at the dawn. Even if such a pool existed,
there was no time for it this morning. She hurried
and was grateful Bylar was prepared with a cloth for
drying.

Kyr was already mounted when they returned to
camp.

"Patu, Ielle-kyr," he said smiling down at her
from the tall beast. She extended her hands to him,
wrists together. He leaned over and quickly secured

44

them in front. Bylar hoisted her up. She sat before Kyr, her legs splayed open wide across the broad back of the animal.

She was to be naked and bound when she entered his lands. That much she could easily discern. It was disappointing, yes, but even the little she knew of him so far, fitting. He would let no one forget that she was property of Kyr of Janos, least of all her.

Makir handed up a large hunk of bread with a kafai milk cheese melted across it. Though it was simple fare, but it would make their morning meal while they rode.

Kyr wrapped his arms around her and picked up the leads. She rested her bare back against him, braced for the bolt forward that always came with the mareshi.

Once again, she centered herself, absorbing the rhythm and after a bit settled into the movement. She was far from comfortable, but so much more so than her position yesterday. He frequently leaned over her shoulder and licked at the spot behind her ear or whispered to her about things he would do to her later, even reminding her of things he had already done. She would periodically raise the bread to him to take a bite and he insisted that she eat her fill as well.

He rested his hands in her lap, holding the reins there and taking the opportunity to fondle between her wide spread legs. She was embarrassingly wet and could do nothing about it. He chuckled against her back every time she squirmed and moaned under his touch.

It was approaching mid-day when she noticed the barren landscape was giving way to farms. They stopped at a tavern to water the mareshi and take a meal. She steeled herself for the experience. It would be much different to be naked in close quarters with these strangers than to have them at a distance. She did know, however, that Kyr would control what happened with his property. She would not be one of the girls that currently knelt tethered by their waist chains outside the tavern door where anyone might use them in any way they wished.

He helped her down and took a moment to kiss her. He stroked his tongue in her mouth, tracing her teeth, enticing her but not ravaging her like the other times.

However he used her she was distinctly aware it was by his choice, never hers. She melted against him, not a solid bone in her body. Her breasts tingled, her core moistened, she could not get enough of his touch. She pressed herself into his shirt and the rough fabric of his pants. She did as much as she could with her bound hands to stroke his chest, wishing they were alone together instead of about to enter this place.

She followed a step behind him, Makir at her side, Bylar flanking Kyr. This town was at the edge of Janos, certainly not a hostile territory, but taverns could become rowdy in the blink of an eye. Bylar would be careful, protective, watching out for trouble.

"Kyr of Janos! How nice to see you again. Our doors are always open to you." The innkeeper bustled about and showed them to a choice table in the corner, giving them the best view of the front door. The furs were soft and plentiful and the men settled on them around the low table.

"Your doors are always open to my coin you mean." The men laughed. It was an old joke between them it seemed.

"You may serve, Ielle-kyr."

She scurried towards the ovens, following the smell of the fresh baked bread and roasting meats.

She collected a tray, looking over the array. She wasn't as agile as she liked with her hands still tied, but at least she was able to serve. It would be beyond embarrassing to have her hands behind her back and a tavern girl serving them. She piled the food on the platter, hoping she had enough for three big hungry men. Just before she was about to start back, she noticed some pakoul berries tucked on a cold shelf. She looked them over, checking for flaws and ripeness and decided to add them for a refreshing surprise to the meal.

47

She walked carefully, holding her tray and dodging the tavern girls. Tavern girls did not mind tripping up an owned girl and making them look bad. There were other owned girls there, yet Ielle was the only one totally naked. Even the tavern girls had shifts that covered them just a bit. They certainly could not bend over without baring all their charms and it was likely a breast would fall out from the sparse bodice any second, but at least they had something. The owned girls glanced sympathetically at her, making her all the more self-conscious.

She paused a moment and closed her eyes, sucking in air, clearing her head and holding herself proudly. She would not be pitied. She was Ielle-kyr of Janos. She wore his chain about her hips, she slept in his furs and serviced him. Clothing or no, she was not one to be looked at in such a way by these other girls.

With renewed resolve, she straightened her back, her breasts thrusting forward with the movement. She caught Kyr's eye across the room, knowing he was watching her every second. She smiled seductively at him, letting her hips sway just a bit, hoping his chain was catching the light. At his table, she bent low and placed the tray on the table before she slipped to her spread knees before him. She assembled a meal for him, decoratively arranging the berries among the rest. She took the plate in her hands, swirling it across her thighs, drawing it up her stomach to her breast, lingering at her heart and kissing the rim. She bowed her head, eyes cast down and offered it to him.

"Your meal is prepared and humbly offered. May it be nourishing and bring you strength."

He took the plate from her, motioning her to continue. She filled similar plates for Bylar and Makir, shifting to face them with her knees together, touching the plate to her forehead and offering to each of them.

"Kyr of Janos offers you this meal. May it feed your body and brotherhood." They took the plates from her and ate heartily.

"To me, Ielle-kyr. You will feed me."

She contained her surprise, for some reason she had not expected that order in this setting. Bylar shifted over a bit so that she could kneel between them. She moved to do Kyr's bidding and unexpectedly found herself tumbled into his lap.

"I might feast on you and the food at the same time." He sucked at the base of her throat causing her to blush and suck in her breath. She caught a glimpse of one of the owned girls, clearly envious that Ielle sat in her master's lap. That bolstered her, allowing her to relax into his embrace, carefully picking which bite he should take next. Once again, he insisted that she eat. "I do not need sickly, tired property, Ielle-kyr. It is

49

your job to take care of yourself as you would take care of me."

She understood but it was hard to eat or think while he was nuzzling her breasts. He took to feeding her between nibbling at her. He grinned when she bit off a yelp, his teeth playing on her skin. He took the final pakoul berry from the plate, holding it in his fingers, locking eyes with her for a moment. He stroked it over her moist skin, coating it with her juices. He smiled at her then pressed it to her mouth. It was sweet from the berry and tangy with her own taste, decadent and wanton.

She was bright red in embarrassment. He took command of her lips again, biting the lower one sharply. She whimpered under his assault then he nudged her legs wider apart and filled her with two of his thick fingers. He sawed them in and out until she could hardly breathe, her chest heaving, her fingers clenching.

He settled his thumb on her, rubbing in sync with his strokes inside her. He moved his mouth to her nipple, chewing at it, flicking it with his tongue. He spoke quietly to her.

"Feel me using you in front of these people, displaying you for my purposes, owning you. Let them hear you, pleading, begging for release, screaming when it comes, Ielle-kyr. Bylar and Makir heard you last night. They heard you this morning. Would you deny these tavern guests? Would you defy me?"

Pithtai worm snake! But by the gods, she was so close. She could not stop the moans and whimpers that slipped from her lips. She could not stop the writhing and thrusting to meet his hand. She tried to hold back, warring with herself against defying him, unwilling to let him take yet another bit of her dignity away. She tried to challenge the voices of her training. She was his. Submit, accept, relax, absorb, find harmony. Those haughty owned girls and tavern maids would hear her. Were probably watching intently right now. Her thoughts raced. Her heat burned. It was no longer her choice, if it ever had been.

The feelings surged, swelled, overflowed and exploded. She spasmed around his fingers, crying out in ecstasy, her hearing clouded, her vision blurred. There was nothing but Kyr and this heavenly feeling flowing through her. Her back arched further, she found herself sucking the skin at his neck, her bound hands clawing at his shirt. Damn him.

He grinned at her, kissing her forehead softly as she collapsed, spent in his arms.

"Good girl. Time to go, up you get." She wasn't even sure she could stand, much less make her way across the tavern to leave. He was wiping his hands then rising to his feet, pulling her up as he did so. She was shaky, her thighs still quivering. She was panting, having not yet caught her breath.

He held her arm, keeping her on her feet as they moved to the door. Other men nodded admiringly at Kyr as they passed.

She could feel her wetness on her thighs. She was mortified, until she caught a look of complete and total envy from one of the girls. Yes, she was Ielle-kyr of Janos, owned property, worthy of being well used.

CHAPTER SIX
~ KYR ~

Kyr felt his happiness well up as the mareshi crossed the wide stone bridge that spanned the Janosa waterway. Home. In his lands again.

The crystal clear waters shimmered in light orange splendor, flowing around the deep blue boulders and light blue of the sandy beaches. There were many lovely places in the world, but the special beauty of his home stood out.

And what could be better than this homecoming. Ielle was cuddled against his chest, languid and relaxed, owned and sated. Oh, she was cross with him too, that he knew. But he loved to tease that fire from her. She would never be indifferent about him.

He brushed his lips along the back of her neck,

tasting her skin and smelling her scent. She stirred then settled again, slumbering in his arms, lulled by the movement of the mareshi and exhausted from serving him.

They would be at his gates soon, but he would let her rest until the last moment. It would be hard for her to be so displayed. Still, she would make him proud, then he would reward her with his use.

Bylar and Makir moved alongside him. Now that they had entered Janos, it was no longer necessary to keep the first watch positions ahead and behind him. He smiled at them both, their brotherhood was a rock that he depended on.

They approved of Ielle. Even though Kyr thought that Bylar had chosen poorly for his own property, he still valued his opinion in such matters. What one could not see for themselves, they were often adept at discerning for others. Bylar was so. Reckless with his own matters, but meticulous and intuitive when it came to Kyr.

When they neared the grounds he knew he could wait no longer. He played his fingers into her lap, stroking and ticking at her mound, dipping his fingers inside her.

She murmured and shifted, slowly rousing until he abruptly smacked the tail of the lead down sharply over her thigh. She bit off a howl, reaching her bound hands to soothe the angry welt. She was cross again, confused, conflicted. Excellent. She would have that mind of hers working full speed as they paraded by his people.

"We are nearly there, Ielle-kyr. Display yourself properly as befits your owner."

She sat up straight, settling her hands under her breasts, pushing them upwards. Her tension returned. No matter. It would help her get through the next bit of time and then he'd strip it from her in his furs.

He sucked at the back of her ear and gently rubbed the welt on her thigh, feeling her shiver at the contrast.

They turned the final corner and entered his grounds, the road lined with his people, waving, cheering, pushing to catch a look at his new property. They grinned and whispered behind their hands, noting her lack of clothing and obvious binding.

When they entered the inner gates, his house staff were all there. The stable master quickly stepped forward to take the mareshi and help them dismount. He jumped down on his own, lifting Ielle off himself, standing her beside him.

His mother stepped forward, taking his face in her hands and tipping his head down to kiss his cheeks. Without a word or motion from him, Ielle slipped to her knees, head bowed deferentially. Good girl. She seemed not to notice or care about the hard stone under her. She held her hands properly under her breasts. No matter how annoyed or uncertain she was, she would yield to her upbringing and training to kneel in deference to his mother.

"Ummi, I present to you my property. Ielle-kyr of Janos," he said, smiling sweetly at his mother.

Ummi nodded to him, accepting the formal presentation, then motioned that he should have the girl rise.

"Up, Ielle-kyr." She rose in that graceful way she had that made his breath catch. There was a sensuous movement about her that was rare and embodied her inner spirit. Refined, subtle, not flashy, but promising so much more. She stood in front of his mother, waiting her inspection.

"Ielle-kyr, I present to you my Ummi. Kaiu-ykir of Janos." She bowed her head to Ummi.

Kyr enjoyed the contrast as they stood face to face. His Ielle naked and exposed, Ummi wearing the traditional dress of a widow, flowing bright green cloth draping her from her shoulders to the ground. He suspected that they might have much in common.

His mother was a formidable woman and she would take the inspection quite seriously.

For many it was just a tradition that they gave a cursory glance to, but it would not be so for his Ummi. She would not hesitate to speak up if the girl was not suitable.

He watched her eying Ielle up and down, walking around her and looking over her backside. She nodded to him.

"Haitu, Ielle-kyr." She bent at the waist, folding double as much as possible, spreading her legs the width of her shoulders. Her intricate braid flipped over her head, dragging on the ground.

His mother ran a hand over the girl's rear end, brushing the nether lips and back of the thighs, then used both hands to measure the hips. Another nod and he gave a word to Ielle to stand straight again.

Ielle's face was flushed. He knew it was much more so from the inspection than from blood running to her head. There were both dried and damp juices on her lower half from his play with her on the way home. His Ummi would not have missed that point, nor would she have missed the welt on the front of her thigh or the patch on her rear that still was a bit pink from his slap last night.

He waited amused for the verdict. Here it was. Ummi turned to face Ielle.

"Welcome to your home, Ielle-kyr of Janos. I wish you much success in your service."

She smiled and took Ielle's face in her hands, kissing both cheeks.

"Kyr," she said turning to him, "I will take her to rest and refresh. Do you wish her to join you for the night meal? Is she to keep these on?" She indicated the ropes binding Ielle's hands.

He considered a moment, knowing Ielle was dying to hear his answer, taking his time and making her wait.

"I will have her at the night meal and those may come off at the bathing." He gave his mother a kiss on the cheek then turned to Ielle.

"Welcome, Ielle-kyr of Janos," he said to her, pulling her against him and then dipping her backwards, her foot coming up off the ground. He stared straight into her eyes, watching all her emotions battle while he held her. The one that was winning was lust. Desire. Heat. For him.

He ran his hand along her side, starting at the swell of her breast and ending at her hip, taking his time playing with the chain at her waist. He spoke quietly against her mouth while he tasted her lips.

"Tonight even my Ummi will hear you scream, Ielle-kyr. There will be no one who will not know how you burn for my touch. There will be no one who will not know you are my property." He grinned at the flash of annoyance in her eyes and grinned even more as it was overtaken with the desperate need for him.

He righted her and slapped her rear, sending her off with Ummi to be introduced to her new home. He had much business to catch up on but also felt the wear of the travel upon him. Beneath it all, he felt rather pleased with himself. His father would be proud he hoped. He was running Janos, the affairs of the house were in order. His lands seemed secure. His Ummi was well cared for and now he had his own property. A property that seemed to be well suited to him.

He retired to his baths, stripping off his clothing and settling into the warm bubbling water of the soaking pools. He bid Bylar and Makir to join him, receiving reports from several of his advisors while he relaxed.

He waved away the servant girls who vied to attend to any needs he may have. There was no call for them with Ielle nearby. He would wait and let Ielle service him later.

She would be wonderful in his furs, pressed against him, wanton and itching for relief. His thoughts wandered a moment, picturing her spread out before him.

"Are you sure you wish to send them away?" Bylar asked, barely trying to restrain a laugh.

"You look in need of attention, Kyr."He glanced pointedly at the rigid flesh between his legs.

"I hope it is not our naked presence that sparks your interest."

Kyr laughed and splashed water in his face. "Shall I call one back for you, Bylar? Or maybe one of the stable boys?"

Bylar grinned. "Fetch Mayia," he called to the servant girls. One scurried off to tend to his request. Kyr laughed heartily, amused to see if Bylar should be able to pay attention to business with Mayia tending to him at the same time.

Mayia-bylar entered moments later, clad in flowing bright red robes. Kyr had to admit she was beautiful, with her dark eyes and night black hair and fairest of skin. Too bad it did not go deep.

She did not have the integrity of his Ielle, not even close to the internal discipline. He knew her to be lazy, scheming constantly for ways to shirk, pouting and sulking whenever Bylar asserted his control.

She was the kind of girl that could be brought to heel if one was to spend all their efforts on it, but to what end? That would leave a man no time or interest for anything else.

Mayia stopped at the edge of the pool, waiting. Yes, lazy. A better girl would enter and beg to serve without being told.

"Naku!" Bylar snapped the command and watched while she removed her robes. She waded through the water to him, waiting again for his order for her to greet him, then again for the order to service.

Kyr sighed. It always made him sad to think of how much more Bylar could have with a better girl. He shrugged away the thoughts. Hopefully Bylar was enjoying her while she lasted. He had no doubts that one day there would be a discard and a lesson learned for Bylar.

They continued to make strategies while Mayia bobbed her head up and down in the water, suckling Bylar then coming up for air. Kyr doubted she was making a great job of it, but Bylar had abstained during their trip, keeping himself on edge and ready for any contingency that might arise.

Four days without release would have him primed quickly, no matter how poor an effort she put in. Bylar had his hands wrapped in her hair, hauling her up to catch a big gulp of air, pulling her back down and holding her against him.

Kyr watched for the moment when Bylar dropped his head back against the side of the pool and closed his eyes, breath blowing out in a steady stream. He quickly took that chance to turn to Makir and begin taking loudly about nonsense, ending with "... and then Bylar will be taking the lead."

Bylar let go of Mayia and she came up sputtering, eyes flashing angrily.

Yes, he timed it perfectly.

Bylar was looking around sheepishly, wondering what he had missed, hoping for a clue so that he did not need to ask. Makir played his part well by nodding in agreement and then saying, "So, you'll be ready to go on time then, Bylar?"

"Yes, yes, of course. Just as long as you're sure that's what you prefer, Kyr. You do not wish to discuss it further first?"

Kyr burst out laughing at the bluff. A fine effort. Bylar quickly realized he was being teased and joined in the merriment. It was good to have these men by his side. Kyr could not ask for a better team.

As usual Mayia was sulking, unhappy at being made to serve at all, much less in this fashion before this audience. Thankfully, Bylar dismissed her and they were able to return to their discussions with renewed focus.

CHAPTER SEVEN
~ IELLE ~

Ielle took a deep breath, readying herself to step out into the hall. The bathing and rest had helped to center her. Kyr's Ummi had been lovely to her, ensuring that she was well tended to and bidding her to call her Kaiu.

Now that she had completed the inspection, Ielle would officially bow to no other female within Kyr's lands, but she still observed a special deference for the past-high woman of the house. It was very pleasing to have not just her formal acceptance but also her blessing.

She knew from the way he held himself at the fulfillment that Kyr was important and powerful but she had no idea he was the Hausa. She never dreamed a

Hausa would travel without a huge entourage. She would take a little time to build her confidence, drawing on her training and trying to apply it to the new reality. It would be enough to run the household of a farmer or shop keeper, or even to be one of many girls in a Hausa's home. To be the first girl of a Hausa was overwhelming. Not just any Hausa either. Janos was a major holding, not some small secluded hamlet.

More importantly, it was amazing to her the Council would even consider such a common girl as herself for him. Even more astounding that he should accept. She came from a good family and was well trained, but certainly was not from a similar standing.

She shook her head and pushed that puzzle from her mind for a later time. She reminded herself that she was smart and would learn quickly. She hoped that Kyr would be patient with her. She would work hard to make sure she did not let him down. She needed all her focus on what she was about to do.

The bells tinkled in the alcove, the signal that the men were entering the hall. She looked at the line of girls, she had yet to meet them all, but knew that the one in the red robes was Bylar's property and the one in the bright yellow was of the stable master.

Kaiu stood at the head of the line, poised to enter first. She would be seated in a place of honor while the rest would line the walls in order by the importance of their men, waiting for the instruction to serve. At the end of the line were house servants who would supply guests or those that had no property of their own available, or even if one of the men should desire additional girls. Tonight Ielle would enter last and provide the entertainment. She took one final deep breath stepping in as the music began.

She moved lightly on her toes, swathed in a diaphanous brilliant blue wrap. The music was deep and melodious, strongly beating like her heart in his presence. It swelled and wrapped around her the same way his arms embraced her.

She caught his eye from across the room, funneling her passion for him into her eyes, pushing everything else away for now, concentrating on no one but him. She whirled around, bringing her arms wide and high, the sheer cloth flying out behind her like a giant wing.

Her naked body shimmered from the lotion that she wore, a dusting of shining fine glitter across her skin. His chain caught the light and sparkled when she moved. She stopped, facing him, arms still high overhead, the veil billowing behind her.

She undulated her body, arching her back, then shifting her hips forward and back. She rolled her shoulders, left and right, making her breasts dance for him, recalling his strong warm hands kneading them, pinching the nipples.

She saw his breath quicken and slowly walked closer to him, her body swaying and rolling. She swirled the cloth in a figure eight, rolling it into a thick cord and wrapping it around her waist several times symbolizing his binding on her. She ran her hands over her torso and breasts, drifting her eyes shut and imagining it was his touch on her skin.

She floated her eyes open to see his smoldering as he watched her. She brought a gentle smile to her lips, knowing he was imagining it too. She unwrapped the fabric, feeding it over her shoulder and then catching the tail between her legs, pulling it up slowly, letting it trail over her sex and between her breasts before repeating the move over the other shoulder.

She moved closer still, her hips rocking and pumping, her breasts bouncing. When she was close enough, she flew the wrap up behind her head again, letting it flow open wide, then bent low and brought it forward, cascading it over his head and shoulders.

She watched his sharp inhale and knew it was covered in her scent. She backed away, teasing it from him then twirling to wrap it around herself. She spun back the other way, letting it go and allowing it to slip sensuously down her body and puddle around her feet.

She picked up the tail, bringing it up into the air in a wide arc, then whipping it down. She moved to one knee, her other leg straight out behind her, her damp sex nearly touching the floor. She bowed her head, pressing her forehead into her knee, arms over her head touching the floor, subjugating herself to him.

She moved again, rising to her feet and holding the see through material in front of her. When she was as close as she could get to him, she took the veil and raised her arms up to the sky, leaning back until her hands touched the floor behind her head, letting the fabric go at the last moment so that it draped over her.

She was perfectly arched, poised for him. She held the position as the last note died around her, then slowly lowered herself to the ground, flat on her back before him.

She was panting, waiting for his verdict on her entertainment, hoping he felt her desire to please him.

He leaned forward and grabbed her hand, pulling her up and shifting her to kneel beside him. He was pleased. Very pleased it seemed, if his erection was anything to judge by.

He clapped his hands and the men motioned for their girls to come to them. They would wait to bring the meal until Kyr was served. He chewed her lip, making her moan, palming her breast and then flicking a nipple before he let her go. He gave her a quick smack on the ass as she moved off to secure his food.

She willed herself not to jump, knowing that left another mark on her that would take some time to fade. She filled the tray from the stores, selecting the best of each item for him, making mental notes about what he seemed to prefer.

When she knelt before him and prepared his meal, the other men sent their girls to do the same. She was focused on Kyr and her task, but she heard the sharp command from Bylar to Mayia. It surprised her, but she made an effort to concentrate on her own work. Still, it crossed her mind that any girl serving the second to the Hausa should not receive such rebuke in public as an ordinary circumstance.

For that matter, it was unlikely a tavern girl serving a stable boy would exhibit such a lapse. Ielle felt shame on her behalf. She would be heartbroken to be found so wanting by Kyr.

The plate complete, she stroked the dish over her skin, across the thighs that already quivered in anticipation of his touch. She crossed the mark from his stripe with the reins, still a bit sore when she touched it, a reminder of his ownership.

She stroked the plate slowly over her skin, rubbing it across the perked nipples, her lips parting and her breath quickening when it moved over her heart and then to her mouth for the kiss. She dipped her tongue out to taste the edge before she kissed it, then dropped her gaze and presented it to him.

"Your meal is prepared and humbly offered. May it bring you warmth and may you find your property pleasing".

It seemed she waited a long time for him to take it. She was tuned to him, she could hear him breathing more heavily than normal. When he took the plate from her, he trapped her hands under his for a moment, stroking them, filling her with promise of things to come. Finally he slipped the dish from her hands.

She looked up and saw his serious look. It brought a smile to her own face to realize he was struggling not to take her right then and there. She was fulfilling her purpose well.

She stayed kneeling at his feet, taking bites of the meal from his hand, sucking his fingers between her lips, stroking them with her tongue. She could see Mayia kneeling beside Bylar. He did not feed her and she was sullen, looking away, pouting her lips, sagging her posture.

She should be trying to win his favor by being completely attentive, eager to please, holding the perfect positions. By the gods, the only thing more shameful than being displeasing in public was to show annoyance at being reprimanded.

She caught Kyr watching her and blushed realizing he was reading her thoughts. There was no thinking that Kyr would tolerate such behavior even if she should lose her mind and attempt it.

Chances were that someone like Kyr would step in even with Mayia should it become any more obvious.

That would embarrass Bylar and therefore embarrass Kyr, but he would exercise control over property within his walls if the owner did not.

Kyr smiled at her, reaching out to stroke her cheek. She nuzzled into his hand, hoping he knew she would never shame him or herself in that way. She put Mayia out of her thoughts and brought all her attention to learning Kyr, watching his movements, logging his responses.

She listened closely to his conversation, not understanding all the details, but enjoying the timber of his voice, his low throaty laugh when the men teased each other causing her stomach to tingle. He pulled her close, resting her head on his knee, stroking his hand in her hair, letting her caress her fingers over his calf while the men told stories.

A house girl served Makir. He was younger than Bylar and Kyr. It may be he was not ready to petition the Council for his own property yet. That was a big decision for the men and most would not want to petition so early that the Council did not grant their request. Makir seemed pleased with the house girl however, as she also nestled against his knee.

Bylar relented and passed the leavings on his plate to Mayia. There was a full meal there but still she sulked that he did not feed her. Kyr looked over and glared, his patience at an end. He snapped a single word in her direction and she quickly scurried back to her place at the wall, kneeling there with her plate, eating alone.

He raised an apologetic brow at Bylar who mere-ly shrugged and continued with his conversation. Ielle's stomach dropped at his anger. She would strive never to have it directed her way. Should it happen, she would do everything in her power to show him her contrition.

She massaged the tension in his muscles, dig-ging a bit deeper with her fingers to try and relax him again. Kyr snapped his fingers at a house girl that so far had not been called to serve. She floated immediately across the room, dropping to her knees before him, legs parted for his pleasure, head bowed, hands on her thighs.

"H- How might I serve you tonight, Master?" she asked softly. Ielle could see she was breathing quickly, excited and nervous to be called by the Hau-sa himself. She could understand that feeling.

"You will spend the night with my friend Bylar, girl. Tend to his needs. Serve him well," he said.

Bylar looked a bit surprised at the presumption, but as a Hausa, Kyr was allowed to take any liberty he liked so he said nothing but his thanks. The girl crawled over to Bylar, kneeling before him. Bylar glanced over at Mayia and Kyr again spoke up.

"Your property will stay put. When you are ready for your furs, I will have her taken there and situated so that she will watch. Perhaps she will learn what it is to serve pleasingly to my brother and the second to the Hausa, eh?"

"As you wish, Kyr," Bylar said turning to appraise the girl at his feet.

"Naku," he said to her.

She shifted on her heels, freeing her simple shift from under her and pulling it over her head, dropping it gently at her side. She slid her hands up to cup her breasts, offering herself to him. Bylar smiled, taking in her naked form.

"To the furs then, girl," he said rising to his feet.

"As you wish, Bylar," Kyr grinned, dispatching one of the young house guards to escort Mayia, giving explicit instructions on how she was to be bound for the night. Tied so that she could not help but hear and see her master take a more pleasing girl. Ielle shuddered at the thought and pressed closer against his leg. He soothed her hair as he talked, then a few minutes later rose to retire to his own furs.

CHAPTER EIGHT
~ KYR ~

Kyr pulled her into his arms, lifting her off the floor as they crossed into his chambers, kicking the door closed behind him. He tossed her onto the soft fur covered pallet that made up his bed and threw himself on top of her.

"Mmmm..." he said, licking over her neck. He inhaled her scent, as always, sunshine and flowers and heat all mixed together.

"You taste delicious, Ielle-kyr."

She squirmed under him, running her hands over his shirt, searching for the hem so that she could wiggle her hands under and caress his bare skin.

"That's tempting, my girl, really. But remember I promised to have you screaming and begging loud enough for my Ummi to hear tonight. And there are doors between us so I have to work extra hard, do I not? Kyr of Janos always keeps his promises, eh?"

"By the gods, Kyr," she said, still fumbling against his shirt. "Do you work so hard just to torment me?"

"I do everything to please myself, girl, don't forget that," he said lightly. She would not know how to take his remark, how to reconcile the tone with the sentiment. He could read her confusion in her eyes.

"If I have the chance to torment you in the process, that is a delightful gift." He took the very tip of her nipple between his front teeth, holding it firmly, tugging until she moaned then giving a bit more pressure until she squealed.

"Yes, there's a nice start, but we'll need much more noise out of you before the night is through, eh?"

She succeeded in working her hands over his stomach, making his flesh tingle. By the gods, he would not be able to hold out long enough if he let her do things like that to him.

He rolled off her. A moment later he had her wrists bound to the corners of his comfy fur covered pallet. Kneeling over her hips he began with her nipples.

Quickly he screwed the two small wooden clamps to them, watching them swell as he increased the pressure. He watched her face closely, seeing her inner struggle. Finally she took a deep breath and let it out slowly. Yes, that was tight enough. He reminded himself that he would have to take care. She would not try to stop him, he must keep his head about him and ensure he did not damage her.

He trailed his tongue along the under-swell of her breast. The softest skin lived there, neglected and lonely. She made those little noises again, something between a whimper and a moan.

He moved to the other side, giving the same treatment then sucking as hard as possible, leaving his mark on her pink skin. She pushed her breast into his mouth, increasing the contact or trying to reduce the pull he was not sure. No matter, either way.

Now that she had passed Ummi's inspection, she would be the high woman of the household and of Janos. Even Ummi would be subordinate to her. The house girls would report directly to her for instruction or discipline, she would determine many household matters, resolve disputes among the girls. He had seen it go to more than one girl's head and he would not have that with his beautiful Ielle.

It was good that she seemed so shocked at that miserable Mayia's behavior tonight. But lest she take it into her head to do something similar one day, he would remind her regularly where her place was. Under him, writhing, moaning, used at his will, as he wished.

He pushed her legs up behind her head, securing them to the wall with another piece of rope. They were spread, her hips up from the bed. She was nervous now, tense, unsure. He massaged her ass with his hands, tracing the marks that lingered from his slaps.

She relaxed, submitting to his will, reveling in his caress, the soft ones and the hard ones. He pinched her lower lips between his fingers, watching to see when she would wince. She groaned finally, probably more than a step past where she wanted to do so.

He traded his tongue for his fingers, laving the spot he had just compressed. So close to her core, so close, but not yet reaching her core. She was twitching, trying desperately to find a way to move her hips but unable to do much in the way he had her bound. She was so beautiful like this. So totally his.

He decided to warm her ass before taking her. It would be a reminder to her all day tomorrow and a sign to all who saw her where her place was. He reached for his sandal, tapping it against his palm to measure it first. Yes, perfect. A suitable sting.

He looked into her eyes, focusing on her intently.

"You please me greatly, Ielle-kyr. I will however, give you reminders so that you continue to do so, eh?"

"As you wish, Kyr. My purpose is to please you."

"A good, proper answer, Ielle-kyr. Very nice. You will scream for your owner, will you not?"

"I am property of Kyr of Janos and I will shout that to the heavens as you wish."

Excellent. He was about to see if the heavens could hear her. Whap. He brought the flat of the sandal down hard. She sucked in a breath and then shouted out his name.

He watched the skin turn a rosy shade. Again and again he brought the sandal down, covering the globes of her ass and tops of her thighs until there was nothing but bright red heat. Tears were running down her face, her voice was going hoarse from crying out her status as his property.

She gasped and screamed, tugging at the bonds on her wrists in frustration, clenching her fingers. Enough. For now. He was so hard and ready, he must take her now. He tossed the sandal aside.

Turning again to lick at her, flicking his tongue over the woman's nub. He sucked at it, tasting her, pulling her higher, making her wonder what would come next, more pain or more pleasure. The delightful mix of the two.

He reached and yanked the clamps off her nipples, her keening wail as loud as any time she screamed his name. He tugged his shirt off and dropped his pants, kicking them away and kneeling between her legs.

"Look at me, Ielle-kyr. Know who owns you."

Her eyes drifted open, locked with his, submitting to him but meeting his challenge.

"I am property of Kyr of Janos. I live to serve him," she whispered roughly.

"Yes, I believe you do, don't you, Ielle-kyr. Good girl." He sank himself to the hilt into her core, watching her gasp then settle into it, tightening her inner muscles around him. He rested his hands on her sore breasts, pinching and twisting the nipples at his whim. The rough hair of his groin pounded into her burning rear, rubbing her thighs.

He thrust, fast, hard, relentless. She gasped and panted, unable to catch her breath, no longer needing air, only needing him. She was tortured by his touch, more tortured if she should not have it.

He released into her, filling her with his hot fluids. He leaned down and laid his teeth onto her nipple. That did it, she tipped over, flexing her inner muscles into him, milking the last drops from him, shuddering and crying, yelling his name again and again.

He freed her legs and arms, cuddling her to him, soothing his hands over her sore rear end. She would be hard pressed to move without pain tomorrow, but she would not forget. He yelled for his chamber maid and a moment later there was a knock at the door.

"Enter," he called.

A light haired girl crossed the room, clothed in a short shift. She dropped to her knees at the side of his bed, head bowed waiting for his orders.

"Ama, bring the balms for Ielle-kyr."

Off she ran, coming back quickly. Kyr rolled Ielle to her side, pressing her softness against his hard naked length, baring her backside to the girl. She melted against him, tensing initially when Ama rubbed the cream into her skin, then ultimately relaxing. He stroked her back, toying with her hair, whispering in her ear. She was his perfect property.

He awoke in the morning with his head pillowed on her breasts. "Mmmm..." He just could not get enough of the taste of her skin. "Good dawn, Ielle-kyr."

She fluttered open her blue eyes, lighting up at the sight of him.

"Good dawn, Kyr of Janos." She rubbed her hands over his bare chest, tracing the body mark on his shoulder with a finger.

"There is much to do today, Ielle-kyr. Ummi will teach you the household duties so that you may run those affairs. You are to do things in the way that you feel they would be pleasing to me, but I would hope you would take Ummi's counsel should she wish to give it."

"Of course, Kyr. Kaiu has much wisdom to offer. I would be a fool to ignore it and a fool not to heed my own voices as well. I would be remiss to show my master has foolish property, would I not?"

"That you would." He sucked a nipple, teasing her while they talked. She flinched when his hands found her ass. Yes, she would be very sore for a while, but she would know she was owned. He loved the heat that radiated off her skin while he pumped into her last night.

"I have business to attend to today, but I will be back for the night meal. Ummi will guide you. You will find your way, will you not?"

"I am good at challenges. I will certainly work until I conquer the task. You would never fear that I might be lazy like..." Her voice trailed off and she bit her lip, unwilling to gossip.

"Good. I see that you see what is and what is not." He gave her a kiss and started to roll away to get ready for the day.

"Kyr," she called. "Might I ask you something?"

"Ielle-kyr, you may always speak freely to me, especially in my chamber. As long as you remain respectful, I will answer you as best I can. You are my property. It goes without saying you will retain my confidences, eh?"

"Oh, but of course."

She seemed flustered he would even think otherwise. He waited, one brow raised, for her to form the question.

"Why did you agree to me? I would not think I would be in line to be the property of a Hausa. I had no idea of your station until we arrived. There are other girls, one would think they are more suited..."

He smiled watching the rush of words tumble from her, more than she'd said to him at once since they met. It was good she was becoming comfortable with him.

"Well," he said, sitting back down, "you know the Council assembles the choices. I do not know how the gods speak to them. I only know that I knew when I saw you that you were for me. I confirmed it during the judging. I saw it reinforced when I brought you to my home."

He caressed her ribs, fingering her skin while he spoke. "I do not want a spoiled child. So many of those girls you would think are for a Hausa would take far too much time and attention. I am a busy man. I want property that is up to that, that represents me well. So far, I am very pleased. You will remain pleasing and the gods will smile."

She was looking softly at him, her eyes welling up a bit with emotion. "Thank you for accepting me," she said, leaning up to take his face in her hands and pull his lips to her own.

"I will do my best for you, Kyr. Always."

81

CHAPTER NINE
~ IELLE ~

"I heard you were pleasing last night." Kaiu's eyes twinkled. Ielle blushed fiercely. Damn him.

"My boy is so like his father. In many ways, I suspect," she looked pointedly at Ielle's bare bottom, still pink and sore from last night. Kaiu grinned.

"A girl is lucky to be chosen for this house. There is nothing better than the service of such men." Her own blush now warming her cheeks.

It was a long day spent learning the workings of the household. There were so many details to attend to. She wondered if she should ever be able to capture them all but Kaiu was encouraging and supportive.

It was afternoon when the house girls lined up before her, kneeling, heads bowed before the high woman of the household. Ielle looked them over, pleased with the collection. There were a variety of girls. Light, dark, taller, shorter, curvy, slim. Something to please any guest.

She frowned however at the randomness of their attire. That would not do for the house of Kyr of Janos. She drilled them through the positions, walking around and making small adjustments to the way they held themselves, demanding perfection for Kyr. There were none that seemed lacking in training or will to serve. This was good.

Ielle smiled looking over the house girls later that evening, lined up in the alcove, ready to enter the hall. They were truly beautiful now. The seamstresses had done great work. Each girl was dressed in sheer fabric, the color specially chosen to compliment her hair, eyes, skin.

The style was the same for each, no longer did they look like a collection of beautiful strays. Draping around the neck, open over the chest, showing the swell of breasts but not entirely bare unless they should move quickly. The skirt brushed halfway down the thighs, swirling softly with every movement. Yes, now they were suitable for the house of Kyr of Janos.

Perhaps it was a small thing, but it was her first mark on the household. She would ensure that Kyr could be proud of everything within her responsibility.

She moved to take her own place in the line, Kaiu stepped aside and motioned her to take the first position.

"No." Ielle shook her head. "You go first, Kaiu. It is right."

"Ielle, you are the high woman now. It is your place."

"My place is at Kyr's feet. The position in line does not change that. You are his Ummi. It is my choice as the high woman and I defer to you on this small point. You will accept my wishes." She held firm, locking eyes with Kaiu. If she was to be first girl of such a house, all the girls must accept her authority.

It seemed to her that Kaiu was going to argue but Ielle would hear none of it. After a moment, Kaiu nodded.

"As you wish, Ielle."

Mayia came flouncing up, pushing her way into the line after Kaiu.

"No, Mayia. That will not be your place." Ielle gave her a steady look, ready to dig in her heels.

"No?

You wish me to move down in the line? I am the owned property of the second to the Hausa. Bylar would be most annoyed if I should not have a place of appropriate standing in the line." Mayia flipped her hair and thrust her breasts out.

"Do you want to disrespect the second to your owner? Do you think Kyr would allow you to do so?"

"You will not attend the line at all tonight, Mayia. You will not attend until Kyr agrees you are allowed." She steeled herself knowing this was a bold move. She had full control over the house girls, but less over owned property. She could not dictate their manner of dress for example. But the line up was within her purview. If Kyr should be displeased, she would take the consequences.

"You will have me out of the line? I can see already what sort of kuckai you are, Ielle. You've barely arrived and already you dare such things?" Mayia eyed her up and down. "You'll be lucky to have only a pink ass after Kyr hears of this. The screams we will hear from you tonight won't be from pleasure anymore."

Ielle flushed realizing that even Mayia had heard her crying out last night. True her rear was still covered in his marks. And Kyr might well be livid at her presumption and the insult to Bylar. But somehow she did not think so. If she was wrong, well, so be it. She would not have Mayia represent the house of Kyr of Janos if she would not even pretend to be pleasing.

"Return to your chambers, Mayia or I will have the house guard escort you."

There was nothing to do now except hold firm or buckle under. She would not give in to a girl like

Mayia. It was time Mayia realized there was a new dawn within these walls. Mayia glared at her but finally decided it was wise to retreat, flouncing off.

As soon as Kaiu was seated, Ielle took her place kneeling before Kyr. She parted her legs, resting her hands on her thighs and bowing her head before him.

"If it should please you, your property would serve you, Kyr of Janos." He stroked his hand over her cheek, drawing her eyes up to him before nodding that she should continue. She could not help but smile at him, happy to be in his presence after being away from him all day. She was learning to read him and there was a definite look of pleasure and desire in his eyes. There was something else too though. Fatigue perhaps. The teasing twinkle did not quite ring true tonight.

She gathered the items for his meal, pleased with her changes there too. She discussed with the cook tastes that were pleasing to Kyr, making sure they were using the finest cuts and cooking them properly. She added items that she already knew he enjoyed that had not been in the offering the night before. Farmers were informed that they were to bring their finest goods directly to Kyr's kitchen for review and possible selection. She had the serving shelves rearranged too. There would no longer be confusion and jostling when the line of girls filled their plates. They were now in an order that matched the way they needed to be selected.

She landed at his feet, filling his plate and following the ritual, hoping with all her heart that her touches were pleasing. She was still learning him so she could not know for sure. She made an effort to slow her breathing, taking a calming breath before putting all her hopes and desires into her kiss to the rim.

"Your meal is prepared and humbly offered. May it refresh your soul and bring happiness to your table."

He took the plate from her. "Where is your girl, Bylar? I do not see her here to attend you."

"Hmmm…" Bylar shook his head." What mischief is she up to now?"

"Kyr, may I please speak?" Ielle looked up at him, her stomach fluttering. For all her bravado to Mayia, she was taking a huge gamble. Soon she would find out if he approved or not.

"You know where Mayia is? Speak up, Ielle-kyr. Is she unwell?"

"No, Kyr. I forbid her from the line up tonight."

"You?" He raised a brow and looked at her quizzically." You. Ielle-kyr. The brand new property. Did not … allow her."

"No, Kyr, I did not." She took a breath and went on. "I told her she is to stay away until you agree to her return. It was not right that she line up with the other girls."

"Interesting. Quite bold of you, Ielle-kyr."

"Yes, Kyr." She watched him considering what action to take. Holding her breath, still unsure how this would go.

"Bylar, your girl will not be attending in the hall for a few days. Please have a house girl to see to you, or I can offer Ielle-kyr for your needs."

Bylar grinned at him. "Mayia will be as furious as a she-cat in a water barrel. That's probably a good thing once in a while. Keeps her from getting too full of herself, no?"

Ielle let her breath out slowly, Kyr did not seem annoyed and Bylar was not disturbed at all.

"I will have a house girl, Kyr, thank you for the of-fer. Ielle can see to you, you take such a lot of special attention after all." The men laughed together, all was well.

Kyr took her to his side and fed her as he ate. On the surface, all seemed as it should be, but still Ielle had a niggling doubt. There was something under-neath that was worrisome to him. She massaged his thigh, rubbing her breasts against the rough surface of his pants, caressing her fingers as high on his leg as she dared, looking at him coyly when he noticed where her hands were. He smiled at her, letting her know he did not mind, playing with her hair and stroking behind her ear.

There was no drama tonight in the hall with Mayia not present. A gorgeous house girl served Bylar. She was wearing the new dress in a fiery bright orange and it suited her perfectly. The men were laughing and joking, the girls were smiling and serving. Kaiu was regal in her place of honor. All was good.

When they entered his chamber, she had a plan in place. She immediately slipped to her knees just inside his door. "Please let me serve you, Kyr. I hope to ease the tension I feel in you tonight and restore you to harmony."

He smiled softly at her and pulled her to her feet, taking command of her mouth, thrusting between her teeth. She pressed into him, her nipples perking and her core heating.

"You're a good girl, Ielle-kyr," he said against her mouth. He massaged his hands over her rear, causing her to thrust her hips against him, his hardness pressing into her.

He walked her backwards to his bed, never taking his mouth from hers. The pallet struck at the back of her knees and she expected him to push her down into it. Instead he twisted, landing on his back and pulling her on top of him. He released her mouth, laughing at her surprise. He smacked a hand onto her flank.

"Get busy, Ielle-kyr. Service your master."

She took her own tongue and trailed it over his lips, playing her fingers in his hair, tracing the shell of his ear with them. He shut his eyes, relaxing under her touch. She sat up, straddling him, leaning back so that she could unfasten his shirt and slip it from his shoulders. He shifted a bit to help her slide it off, smiling as he watched her work. She took her mouth and kissed at his body mark, following it over his skin with her moist touch while she teased her fingers over his hard chest.

She flicked her tongue over his nipple, watching it harden then sucking at it, hearing him moan. He stroked his hands over her bare back and down onto the sore cheeks, kneading, clenching, releasing. She trailed her tongue down and swirled it around his navel, unable to help her grin when he twitched under her. She reversed her position, shifting so that she straddled his chest facing his feet while she took her time working at the waist of his pants.

She moaned loudly when he leaned up and licked across her ass, tracing some of his marks while she played her fingers low over his torso. He shifted so she could push his pants down, kicking them free of his feet. She eyed his hardness, tall and ready, fingers kneading high on his thighs while she planned her attack.

A swath of her tongue over his skin, below his navel, but not yet touching his cock. A groan from him. She smiled to herself. She flicked her tongue over the tip of his hard cock, rewarded with his shudder. He pulled her hips closer to him, holding her in place, using his tongue on her as she did on him.

She moaned when he flicked it along her slit, retaliating by bringing her tongue from the base to the tip. She cupped his sack in her hands, gently massaging, then flicked the head again. Ah, by the gods! He had latched on to her woman's nub, sucking hard, relentlessly at it. She caught her breath, trying to think and remember what she was doing.

Ielle engulfed him into her mouth, sucking him as deeply as possible, paying him back for the delicious things he was doing to her. She teased her tongue over him, working into a rhythm and bobbing her head up and down on him. She took him in as far as she could then came as close to the tip as she could before thrusting her mouth back down to the bottom again.

She dueled with him, quickening her pace, then slowing. Matching what he was doing to her. She was finding it impossible to get ahead of him, even in this position he was still in charge, still driving while she followed.

She could feel how close he was, she readied herself to receive him in her mouth, when he slapped her ass and barked out, "Bartu, Ielle-kyr."

She dropped him from her mouth reluctantly but moved quickly to take the position, ass up, head down on his furs. He settled behind her, leaning over her to take her breasts in his hands, squeezing and massaging them roughly.

He bit gently at her shoulder, then pinched harder with his teeth and slotted himself into her. He pounded her, working out his tension, rolling the nipples between his fingers. She held him as tightly as she could, focusing her energy on receiving him for his pleasure.

She heard herself moaning, wailing then the waves broke over her body, sensations converging and shattering around her. He pumped several more times then quivered and began to spurt into her.

He pulled away and she felt overwhelmingly empty at the loss. A moment later, she realized he finished by spraying across her ass. He released her breasts and massaged her rear instead, working the fluids into her skin like a balm.

When he was done, she crawled up to him, laying on his chest, stroking her fingers over the body mark, pressing kisses into his chest from time to time.

"You're a good girl, Ielle-kyr. I am pleased with your touches on the household. Ummi has kept things right and proper but it takes the loving and wise moves of owned property to bring that special spark, eh?"

She lit up with pleasure, so delighted he was happy with her direction.

"I hope I did not overstep with Mayia."

"That was wise. She may sit out for a bit and learn a lesson."

He soothed the bruise his teeth left on her shoulder, gently pressing into the skin.

"Your light does not quite reach your eyes tonight, Kyr." She turned her head to watch his face. He smiled softly at her, dropping his lips onto her nose in a teasing touch.

"Are you a mystic, Ielle-kyr?" he asked. "I would not think most would know me that well so quickly."

"I am not most. I am for you." She smiled at him. "Totally, completely. There is no one else that has my attention as you do. I am studying, learning you." She brushed a finger over his forehead. "There is a slight deepening of the line here."

She moved her hand to his eyebrow then along the side of his eye. "And a twinkle that is missing here."

She stroked down across his upper lip. "And the barest of frowns that settles here."

She laughed when he unexpectedly sucked her finger into his mouth, stroking it with his tongue a moment, reminding her deliciously of where that tongue had recently been.

"You are a bright girl, Ielle-kyr. Yes, there are some troubling words in the wind. There are always forces that would de-seat a Hausa, but there are whispers that someone inside my walls may wish it so."

She gasped, nearly unable to absorb such a thought. A Hausa required the best of the best. That someone could come into his walls with such a thought was incomprehensible.

"Do not worry, my girl. We will weed out any traitor."

He was quiet a moment, gently stroking her while she watched his thoughts turn. As though he flicked a switch, she could see that talk of this topic was closed and he came back with the twinkle that was nearly as it should be.

He gave a swat to her behind that made her jump. "Ummi says she heard you were pleasing last night."

CHAPTER TEN
~ KYR ~

Kyr shifted on the mareshi, careful not to let his attention wander too far. Although he was an expert rider, the mareshi were volatile animals and it was not wise to lose focus on the trail. Still, it plagued him that there could be someone in his house who would try to remove him. It caused him to look at everyone with a wary gaze. He should not have to feel watchful in that way in his own lands, much less his own home.

He had spoken with many of his allies, carefully dancing around the topic at hand. None seemed to have any inkling of the situation, none seemed to be involved. It was hard to know if they told the truth. He did not think they lied, but obviously he had someone within his own walls who lied daily and he did not see it. How could he trust that he would know the liar when he found them?

Unfortunately, he had good confirmation of the rumor. His mystic came to him independently, speaking of a vision of a snake in the grass, slithering silently, poised to strike. He must take all care and flush the traitor quickly. Bylar, Makir and the rest of his closest advisors were methodically working to find the one that would betray him, but so far, to no avail. It had been a full moon and he was becoming frustrated.

The joy he usually felt when crossing the bridge over the Janosa waterway was tempered. The beauty still struck him, but now he wondered what lingered under the surface. His happiness did swell knowing that Ielle would be waiting for him. He had been gone two days and truth be told, he missed her warmth in his furs. Not only because he had not availed himself of the girls provided by his hosts in the nearby lands, but also because her spirit enticed him and her wisdom interested him.

She was kneeling on the stones waiting for him when they entered the gates. Her dark hair cascading down her bare back, her head bowed, hands on her parted thighs. As soon as he allowed her up, she threw herself into his arms with genuine warmth and abandon. He laughed and tipped her backwards, nibbling over her neck and down to catch a breast between his lips until she moaned. "I see you are well, Ielle-kyr."

"And you too, Kyr of Janos," she answered, brushing her thigh against his groin. He laughed again and stood her on her feet. He loved what a wanton girl she had become with him. She still embarrassed easily, making her delightful to tease, but he enjoyed the way she had become more comfortable with him since the last moon.

He took her to his furs, determined to use her well and make up for the time he was gone. He started by securing her hands to the top of his bed.

"I have been tormented for days without you, Ielle-kyr. It only seems right I should torment you in return, does it not?"

"Yes, Kyr."

"Hmmm… Let's see. Ah! I have not used these in some time, have I?" He got out the wooden clamps. "Beg for them, Ielle-kyr."

"Please, Kyr, use your property. I have missed your touch, missed your scent, missed your presence." She spread her thighs wide for him, inviting him to use her.

"Well, that wasn't much of a beg really, but I'll be accommodating, just this once." He fastened one on her right nipple, tightening it until she gasped. She sucked in her breath, tensing her body in response. He flicked at it, watching her squirm and hearing her moan.

"And what might I do with this second little toy, eh?"

"Anything you like, Kyr."

"Yes, anything I like. I am your owner, you are my property, are you not?"

"Yes, Kyr. I am totally yours." He trailed the wooden piece over her skin, stroking it between her breasts, tracing it on her thigh.

"Stick your tongue out, Ielle-kyr."

She looked puzzled but complied. He fastened the clamp on the end of her tongue, not painful, but secure, annoying, he was sure. A reminder that she was his to do with as he chose. He left her a moment, pulling something from his things.

"I was given this interesting oil while I was traveling. I think I should try it on you, Ielle-kyr." She nodded, not really in a position to answer him properly. He poured a bit onto her stomach, watching it pool and run. He rubbed it slowly into her skin, kneading it into the breast that he had not clamped. He waited to see when it might take effect.

There it was. She was moaning. It warmed and tingled on her skin. He smoothed it over her belly, using a finger to take it along the crease of her thighs. He poured more across her mound, watching it drip along the cleft of her lips. She was rocking her hips, her feet kicking.

He massaged it into her skin, fondling her

mound, playing with the small tuft of hair that remained there. He poured some on his fingers then watched her face while he worked two into her sex.

Hot, wet, tight. How he loved feeling inside her. Her eyes were dark blue, heavy, languid, enjoying what he was doing to her at the same time she squirmed and wiggled under the tingle and the heat.

She stifled a yelp and bit her lip when he plucked the clamp from her breast, shifting to a moan when he worked the skin roughly. One hand on her breast, one hand pushing fingers into her sex, she was writhing under his touch. He felt her inner muscles press against his fingers, her thighs tensing. He took the clip from her tongue and her voice was breathy when she thanked him.

"Please, please use your property, Kyr. I tingle and burn for you, inside and out. Please." He smiled.

"Turn over, Ielle-kyr. I should get your backside as hot as your front, eh?" She whimpered when she turned, but did so immediately. He caressed his fingers over her rear, feeling the skin there, enjoying the tight muscles under the softer padding.

She gasped and tensed when he brought the dozen tails of the short leather whip down on her skin. He watched the lines appear. He had not smacked her harshly, just enough for her to feel the sting and leave a sign that she owned. He rubbed his hand over her skin, feeling it, caressing it, soothing it. She relaxed and became pliant, then he struck again. She jumped but did not cry out this time. He returned to running his hands on her skin, letting the softness permeate her body. Then a stroke. Back and forth, until she was raising her ass off his furs to press into his lashes. Moaning with the feeling but begging silently for more.

His touch on her, his marks on her. There was nothing more beautiful than owning her and having the evidence before him. He rubbed between her thighs, feeling the moisture, pulling her up and then slotting himself inside.

He used her, possessed her. She absorbed him, clenching tightly against him while he moved in her. He tensed, his power surging then spilling inside her. The release washed over him, waves throbbing through his body. He gulped for air, realizing he had been holding his breath.

She licked him clean, teasing him with her tongue. She was still needy and wanting, and she begged him with her eyes. She had not had her own release. He left her that way, stroking her back and hair, leaving her need as a reminder that she was owned property, mastered, his. They lay together, she gently licked at the sweat on his skin. He pulled a fur over them to keep her from chilling.

"By the gods, I do not know what it will take to find this snake! There is no one who even seems to know for which hostile faction he works. It is beyond frustrating, Ielle-kyr. Every day my anger grows and when I find this man, he will suffer deeply." She shivered at his tone and he took a deep breath to calm himself again, not wanting to bring back the tension Ielle had just released for him. He played with her hair, feeling it float between his fingers, re-laxing him again.

"Obin of Mashet will be coming soon. You must be prepared to entertain his retinue, Ielle-kyr. I would expect you to represent the house of Kyr of Janos well."

"Of course."

"His mystic will attend him. Perhaps he will see something that ours cannot." His fingers tensed and released. He made another conscious effort to try and relax but it was difficult. Kyr's people had held Janos for generations. He could not be the one to allow it fail. He could not stand to have his house dispersed, his loyal staff sold off at auctions. He must not allow such a thing and yet someone within his walls wished it.

Ielle caressed him, reminding him of his vow not to tense tonight. "Is there a way to draw him forth? A ruse of some kind? If they should think you were ill, maybe that would bring them out to strike."

"Hmm... perhaps." He tweaked her nipple mak-ing her yelp. "Ama!" He yelled for his chamber maid. As soon as she entered the room he dispatched her to bring Bylar. It was an excellent idea. They could lie in wait and capture the criminal. It was unexpected, a woman's way, sneaky and clever. Not a man's way of force and might. But force and might was not working. Perhaps it was wise to try something no one would anticipate.

He looked at her kindly. She was so soft against him, caressing and massaging him. She was quick. That was a sure benefit to him, but it would not do to let Ielle become too full of herself. She was smart enough to turn that to her advantage if he should allow it.

Bylar entered, wearing only his pants, shrugging on his shirt as he walked, clearly roused from his furs. Ama quickly made to prepare a seat for him, kneeling to the side should they require anything else of her.

"Kammu, Ielle-kyr." She moved quickly but he caught the look of shock in her eyes. Good. It threw her off to serve him in front of Bylar. It shook her even more in front of the chamber maid. She was still wanting from his denial of her release. She would not begin to think that she wielded the power.

Ielle crept down to his lap, settling herself between his legs, looking up at him and kissing the tip of his cock. She licked her tongue up the sensitive underside, flicking along the way. He worked his fingers into her hair while he told Bylar of the idea.

"Trickery and deception! Very nice, Kyr." Bylar was thinking aloud about details. Kyr heard him but more and more of his attention was focused on the spirals Ielle was making with her tongue, teasing from the base to the tip. He was fully hard now and he could not help but shudder when she engulfed him. Her warm, wet lips, soft and snug around his hot throbbing skin. He tightened his hands in her hair, moving her head as he desired. He let go of thoughts of the plot and pumped his hips up into her mouth. All of his being centered on release, primal heat taking him over.

She was cupping him, fondling him gently, driving him further and further towards the edge. She stroked a finger over that sensitive bit of skin between his balls and his ass, nearly causing him to come unglued. He steadied himself then in one final thrust, let go, filling her mouth with his fluids.

She backed off and switched to feather light brushes of her tongue on him, licking every bit from his skin. He stopped her from wiping some from her chin. "No. Leave it, Ielle-kyr. It is another of my marks on you. You should see how lovely your ass looks with my stripes on you." She took a deep breath, centering herself again probably. She remained in his lap, licking and sucking gently at the skin of his thighs and groin.

"So do you think we can be successful, Bylar?" Kyr asked, getting back to the point at hand.

"Oh, yes, yes. We will need to keep this quiet of course. Ama, you will speak of this to no one do you understand? Should I discover such a thing I will have you discarded as a traitor."

Ama actually shivered at his words. Good. She had been a trusted servant in his house for some time, specially chosen to serve him in his chamber where she might be privy to any sort of confidences. Until this latest crisis he had no reason to ever suspect her of anything. He hoped his trust was well placed. It seemed from her reaction it was.

They would put the plan in place sometime in the next few days. Bylar would secure a potion that would simulate a severe illness but in fact, it would be merely pretense. While he lay on what appeared to be death's bed, with any luck, there would be an attempt upon him. He would be primed and ready to respond, the traitor would be flushed out and all would be well again. Excellent.

CHAPTER ELEVEN
~ IELLE ~

Ielle woke to Kyr's hand in her hair and his mouth on her breast. She stretched sinuously under him, working her fingers over whatever part of his skin she could reach.

"Obin of Mashet will arrive today. I am pleased with the improvements you have made for the visit. So much in fact, that I am going to have you adorned for the occasion."

"Oh Kyr, thank you!"

How exciting to think that she would have some sort of decoration besides her own skin and the various ways the chamber maid found to braid her long hair. It had been so long. She could hardly remember how it felt to wear any clothing, or for that matter even what it was to enhance her lips with rouge. She did not think that his adornment would include anything along the lines of an actual gown, but whatever it was, it would be something more than she had available for so many weeks.

He distracted her train of thought by nudging his finger between her lower lips, trailing it across the warmth. Moisture gathered there, she was moaning softly. He was teasing, brushing so softly, pulling back when she tried to push her pelvis into his touch, never letting her generate quite enough pressure. It was a tantalizing torture, driving her crazy while he played with his teeth on her nipple. He looked up and grinned at her.

"I think I should not do all the work when I have my owned property right here, Ielle-kyr. Up you get. Stand before me and pleasure yourself while I watch."

By the gods, it was one torment after another with him, was it not? But a pleasurable torment none the less. She slipped to her feet, her skin flushed while he shifted himself on the furs and settled back to watch her.

She began by licking a finger, sucking it into her mouth, stroking her tongue over it like a child's candy, imagining it was his skin she was tasting. She watched him, putting her passion into her half-closed eyes, drawing him in, letting him know she performed for him alone.

She kneaded her breast with the other hand, giving a small gasp when she pinched the nipple tightly, the way he would do. She took the finger from her lips, tracing the small tuft of hair at the base of her mound before dipping it into the top of the cleft. She slid it along the path he had traced earlier, gathering her juices then returning it to her mouth to lick them clean. Her nipples were perked, her skin was warm, she was soft and wanting.

She dropped into a squat, as open before him as ever possible. She slipped her finger inside, feeing the warmth there. She was temping to close her eyes but she kept them locked with Kyr's. She watched the pulse at the base of his throat start to quicken.

She pulled her finger out and circled it over her nipple then jammed two fingers back inside, noting his sharp intake of breath. She rubbed her other hand across her mound, then used it to ensure her lower lips stayed wide open while she worked herself on the other hand. Her thighs and calves were tiring from the position but she held it, knowing it was exciting him to see her thus. She brought a hand back to the nipples, tugging them out from her body, imagining it was his hand on her skin as she did so.

She worked her thumb onto on her most sensitive spot, stroking it every time her fingers entered her core. Ah, yes, that was exquisite. She flicked it sharply, gasping when she did so, knowing he'd enjoy seeing her do it. She slapped her hand onto her flanks, flinching at the self-induced sting, the pop reverberating in her ears.

He twitched watching her and took his manhood in his own hand, stroking it idly with his own fingers. She was so close now, riding on the edge, for some reason unable to quite manage to tip over.

She dropped her knees to the ground, releasing the growing burn in her thighs, shuffling herself as close to his pallet as possible. She continued to work at herself, thrusting her fingers, pumping against them, teasing her nipples.

"Please Kyr, please, use your property." By the gods, she needed him so desperately.

She longed to take his hard cock in her hand but did not dare to touch until he should allow her to. Her nipples were so hard, so needy, she was so hot and wet, her fingers were slick and moisture rubbed her thighs. She was breathing fast, close, so close.

He scooted to the edge of the furs, using his hands to pull her to him. He rubbed his cock against her thigh, close, so close to where it really needed to be. She moaned, still stroking herself as he instructed, still playing with her nipple for him. She pushed her breasts forward, practically in his face, hoping he would be enticed by them.

He snaked out a tongue to the skin of her chest, but deliberately stayed away from the nipple that she so wanted him to suck. He grabbed her wrist, moving

it for her, speeding up the pace of her strokes, intensi-
fying the force, slamming it into her. He took her other
hand and pressed her fingers tighter onto the nipple,
twisting and turning.

She was panting and moaning, then screaming
with her release, her bud painful now with the pressure still applied. It seemed forever before he released her hand from her crotch and her fingers from
her nipple, laying her down on the bed and pulling
her breast into his mouth.

He stroked her thighs, played with the small tuft
of fur at the junction of her legs.

Suddenly, he was shoving himself into her. She
was so focused on her own pleasure she had nearly
forgotten he was hard and ready.

She struggled to make up for her lapse by meeting his thrusts with abandon, clenching as tightly as
possible on him, sucking at his chest, flicking her
tongue on his nipples. They pebbled under her
mouth and watched his eyes glaze over.

He shuddered and thrust one last hard time, hitting deep inside her while he exploded, collapsing on
top of her, panting. He laid on her, staying inside her
as long as he could. She nuzzled into him, stroking
his hair and shoulders, caressing and licking, inhaling his scent. There was nothing better in her world.

It was much later that she attended to the bathing pools with the rest of the girls. She sat down in

the water and rested her head against the edge, closing her eyes and letting the warmth of the bubbling water swirl around her with the chatter of the bunch.

Mayia returned to the lines after some time and there had been no more drama in the dining hall. Her attitude was still poor, her tongue too biting and free among the girls, but at least she kept that at bay when Kyr was around. Perhaps she did learn something.

Mayia had never spoken of that night Kyr rebuked her, but the chamber maid had let loose many of the details. While Ielle made a point not to engage in gossipy conversations, she could not help but hear the description. Perhaps she enjoyed it a bit too much even.

A cold stone phallus inserted, then legs lashed together to hold it in place. Made to stand at the foot of Bylar's furs, arms bound tightly overhead, unable to do more than squirm. Bylar took the house girl over and over, screaming on his furs. Mayia could not even close her eyes and pretend to be elsewhere. Anytime she tried to look away, the chamber maid was to give her a sharp cut with a narrow switch.

It seemed the chamber maid enjoyed Mayia's comeuppance even more so than most, having been the recipient of many of Mayia's tantrums over time. Whether it was a good chance for revenge, or Mayia was just slow to learn and obey, they could not know, but Mayia certainly bore the evidence of dozens of strokes with the switch. Thin red lines crisscrossed her breasts, back, thighs, even her stomach and took days to fade away.

Mayia had been left to stand there all night, practically on top of the sleeping master and the girl that pleased him more than she did. Ielle could not imagine the pain of such a punishment. She would gladly take a hundred whippings than to be faced with being found so displeasing. She really hoped that Mayia had learned from it all, but worried that instead someone like Mayia would let it feed her lack of character, rather than make a noble change.

Bells chimed and Ielle was brought back from her thoughts. Obin of Mashet would be nearby. They must hurry and dress. Two chamber maids appeared with a long coil of deep blue rope, the thickness of Ielle's finger. She was bid to hold her hands out of the way behind her neck while they wrapped her in the cord. Several times they consulted a page of instructions from Kyr to ensure that they were draping the rope as he wished.

It diamonded across her torso and around her breasts, wrapping her like Kyr's arms around her skin. It was snug, but it did not cut into her skin or hamper her breathing. It was his touch on her body. When they were ready, she brought her arms down and they completed the same pattern down both arms and legs. She was covered from neck to ankles, yet not covered at all. There were spaces the size of her fist between each square. The blue color reflected in her already deep blue eyes, making them pop from her pale pink skin.

Two strands ran between her legs, bisecting her lower lips. They were quite snug if she bent or squatted, rubbing at her in a provocative way. A knot was strategically placed to press into her sex, designed to keep her tremendously aware of herself. The final touch was rouge to her nipples and lips, brightening their color. The rope binding already enhanced their prominence on her chest, thrusting them outwards, perked and ready for use.

"By the gods, Ielle," one of the girls said, "You are a credit to the house of Kyr of Janos."

They lined up around the courtyard, kneeling on the stones, eyes cast down, waiting for the visitors to arrive. The binding dug into her core with every breath, causing her moisture to gather between her thighs. Kyr watched her from afar. She swore she knew every move he made even when she could not see him. Obin arrived within the gate, the mareshi dancing to a halt. They were met by stable hands and dismounted, their girls kneeling beside them while greetings were made with Kyr and his men.

"Obin of Mashet, I present to you my property, Ielle-kyr of Janos. She shall see to your women when you are ready to release them." Kyr touched her shoulder, letting her know she should now stand. She rose to her feet, settling her hands under her bound breasts, hands clasped together.

Obin stepped forward, sharply flicking a finger across her left nipple. She fought the urge to flinch or cry out, pleased that she betrayed herself with only a small twitch.

"She is quite lovely, Kyr. One hopes she is pleasing in the furs."

"Should I keep her if she were not?" Kyr replied lightly. Ielle noted that small tightening of his jaw that betrayed his easy manner. Typically, a man would receive permission before fondling owned property. Given the chance, it was likely Kyr would offer her to an honored guest, perhaps even for his full use. She wondered if Kyr would be so inclined now.

She escorted Obin's girls to the baths and rest area where they mingled with the girls from the house of Kyr. She played the hostess, chatting amiably with the girls, ensuring that they had food and drink while they bathed. It was a bit disappointing to see Bata-obin seem to take a shine to Mayia. They giggled and laughed together, finally wandering off to talk among themselves. She hoped Mayia would behave herself with the guests. She was confident Kyr would not tolerate any embarrassment in front of company.

"Bata-obin, would you like to come and see the hall? I would be happy to show you where things are." It would soon be time to serve the men.

"Ielle, always the master. Telling everyone what to do. We are having a lovely time talking. What does she really need to know?" Mayia pouted and rolled her eyes.

"I'm sorry to disrupt your confidences. It is your choice of course, but if you choose to, now is the time." Ielle deliberately ignored Mayia's childish behavior.

Bata looked back and forth between the two then broke out in giggles. "Mayia! She really is as you claimed. By the gods!"

"Oh yes, you should see her. She is so jealous of me that she can't stand it." Mayia cupped her own breasts, weighing them in her hands showing how they ran well over.

"Look at her. She's half the size I am. She can't measure up the way I do. It makes her crazy. She made Kyr leave me out of the line up for days and days. She shakes those little breasts of hers and wiggles her ass in his face and he will do anything she wants."

"Mayia!" Ielle reached out and slapped her. She would not have any girl speak so of the Hausa.

Mayia launched herself at Ielle, knocking her breath from her when she landed backwards in the furs. Mayia straddled her hips, grabbing a hold of her nipples, pinching them viciously. Ielle struggled to push her off, trying to grab Mayia's hands.

Mayia glared at her and twisted, making her cry out. "You may rule Kyr, but you do not rule me, Ielle."

Ielle sucked in her breath, marshaling her strength despite the pain. She twisted to the side, knocking Mayia off balance enough to dislodge her. That's all it took for her to get the upper hand. Ielle pushed her face down into the furs, throwing herself across Mayia's shoulders, pinning her in place.

She reached a hand back and slapped it soundly on Mayia's rear, leaving stinging handprints in her wake. Mayia kicked and screamed but Ielle did not stop, paddling her like a small child.

Ielle yelped, finding herself hauled off Mayia. The house guard was there, pulling her up by the ropes that adorned her, making the knot at her core dig into her savagely. He let her go and yanked Mayia up even more abruptly.

"Girls, girls!" The guard held Mayia who was red faced and still screaming incoherently. Ielle backed out of reach and tried to catch her breath, her body covered in a sheen of sweat from the struggle.

"Haitu, Mayia, perhaps that will clear your head. Move now or I shall have to help you with my strap." Mayia stamped her foot then grudgingly shifted to the position, spreading her legs and bending double. She was still cursing Ielle but not as loudly.

"Silence, girl!" He pinched her lower lips tightly until she yelped. "Do I have your attention now?" he asked.

"Return to your chambers and prepare to serve, Mayia. The bell will be ringing soon." He turned to the rest of the girls. "Tend to your duties. Ielle, I assume this matter is ended?"

"Yes, thank you. It is just a small disagreement among property, nothing of importance." She would not keep it a secret if they should ask, but she saw no reason to tattle to Kyr or Bylar.

She was relieved when the bell rang signaling time to line up for the dining hall. The less time Mayia spent with Bata, the less time she would have to get herself into trouble.

CHAPTER TWELVE
~ KYR ~

Obin was such an ass. There was just no other word for him. Yet politics required that Kyr entertain him. How was it that someone so annoying ended up with such a strategic stronghold? Ah well, the comedy of the gods was not for them to understand.

It surprised him that he felt such a strong reaction to seeing Obin fondle Ielle. It was a huge lack of respect not to secure his leave first. She was his property and there was no excuse that Obin would be confused on that point.

Obin was such a simpleton that he probably intended no offense to Kyr. He was undisciplined and reacted impulsively, speaking without thinking, taking whatever caught his eye like a child. That made his strategic location all the more precarious and caused Kyr and the others of his allies to court him all the more closely. Obin could easily switch allegiances over a shiny rock or a piece of candy.

Of course the more they indulged him the worse he got. An endless circle. One day Obin would come crashing down. Kyr just hoped he was far away when it happened and that the impact did not fall among Kyr's lands.

Obin droned on while he pretended to listen. There was something more to it than just the respect for him as a property owner. Obin's hand on Ielle's nipple hit him like a kick to his gut. It was visceral, he was fiercely protective in a primitive way.

He loved the power of knowing that he was the only man to make Ielle twitch and thrash, beg and plead for release. He did not want another's hands on her. It was Ielle. His Ielle. Only his.

Something else too though. Tenderness for Ielle. Yes, she definitely held a special place with him. He trusted her completely, she knew him most intimately. It was the unique bond of owned property. It was not something he planned to share anytime soon.

Kyr watched the girls file in, arranged in two lines side by side. Ummi led the list, crossing the floor and settling into her spot, followed by Ielle and Obin's girl, each of them taking their places with their masters. The rest of the girls split right for the house of Kyr and left for Obin, lining the walls, waiting for the signal to join their owners.

He nodded to Ielle to begin her service, enjoying the way she looked in the bright blue ropes. He would keep her in those for a good long time, perhaps he would try other colors now and then. The rouge on her nipples made them all the more fetching, apparently enough that Obin forgot his manners with her. It was not the first time he had seen him do something similar. Obin would not take any further liberties with Ielle-kyr of Janos though. She was his. He would decide who would play with her and under what circumstances.

It was polite for him to notice Obin's girl, but truthfully he had no time for her. She was young and flighty, although he would admit, pretty enough, with long brown locks and delicate features. Her breasts were a bit small for Kyr's taste, but it was mostly her childish air that annoyed him. Obin had offered her to him the last time he visited Mashet, but he had demurred just because he couldn't be bothered. He watched Ielle and the other girl at the serving counter, working side by side, Ielle suggesting treats and delicacies to the girl for presentation to her master as an honored guest. Good girl. She was an excellent hostess. He would be proud to have her represent his home to other visiting Hausas.

The girls made their way back to Kyr and Obin. He watched the two of them. Obin's girl was obvious and blatant, wigging her rear and shimmying her breasts while she moved across the great hall. Ielle was elegant and sensual. Even though she was all but naked, she came off with an aura of refinement and nobility. His chain flashed on her hips, sparkling with her movement. Obin's girl, for all her flowing robes and finery, came off cheap and crude.

Ielle was before him. Her legs parted so that he could see the double strand of rope running between her legs. The knot was perfectly placed and he could see by the sheen between her thighs the effect it was having on her, especially when she did things like kneel and bend. Her hands were so soft and delicate, carefully selecting each perfect morsel for his pleasure.

She moved his dish over her thighs, tracing it over the ropes that he bound her with, sliding it over the soft curve of her stomach, swirling it across her heart. She caught his eye when she pressed it to her breast, her affection and devotion to him shining from her. She kissed the rim passionately, then made the offering. "Your meal is prepared and humbly offered. May it bring you refreshment and honor your house."

He took it from her, imagining those same passionate kisses on his skin later. Remembering those lips on him just this morning in his furs. He patted his knee to indicate she could attend by his side and motioned to the men that their girls may now serve.

He ate bites of the meal, periodically feeding

some to Ielle, her mouth on his fingers when she leaned in to sup from his hand. Obin went on at some length about farming and crops and he pretended to pay attention, knowing that any topic Obin was on about was rarely important. Obin mostly just enjoyed the sound of his own voice.

Fortunately Bylar kept up with the conversation, sharing anecdotes and making jokes. His girl was back in the dining room now, much more subdued since that day he had her punished. He had no doubts she was still as big a waste as always, but at least she had learned to keep it from his sight and hearing. He noticed her cheek and her rear end were both bright pink. Interesting. Perhaps Bylar had taken her in hand recently.

He caught Bylar's eye and raised a questioning brow towards Mayia and then Obin. Bylar just shrugged, it was of no importance to him. Excellent. That would serve several purposes for the night.

"If it should please you, the entertainment is ready," Ielle said softly from his side. He smiled down at her, wondering what she may have come up with for their guest. She was smiling brightly, excited to show him what she had organized. Kyr clapped his hands and three of the house girls took their places in the middle of the room.

The music began and the girls started to undulate, stroking each other, sliding limbs together then

apart. Their sheer costumes moved and shifted, float-
ing softly around them in the bright colors that Ielle
had selected. One yellow, one orange, one red, they
moved as though they were flames in a torch, touching each other, arching backs. Rounded swells of
breasts flashed then receded under the low flowing
necklines, rear ends peeked and hid as the skirts floated and swirled.

The dance built and the heat of the flame grew.
The girls had their hands inside each other's clothing
now, kneading breasts, palming ass cheeks. Ielle
played her fingers quite high on his thigh, connecting
her touch to the living sculpture before them. His
cock hardened, delightfully entranced by the chore-
ography Ielle had arranged. The tops of the dresses
fell, breasts now completely naked, girls rubbing
their chests against each other, glimmering and
shimmering with some sort of sparkling oil. Hands
and mouths were everywhere. Taut nipple buds
were licked and sucked. He could see the flash of
teeth as they pulled back from each other, writhing,
moaning.

Hands on ass cheeks, fingering the flesh, pressing
into the skin. Ielle pressed into his thigh in a similar
way, making his pulse quicken. He rested his hand on
her shoulder, fingering the cords that crossed it, wiggling and nudging at them knowing there would be a
tightening and rub against her in return. Skirts were

off, hands holding them high in the air, twirling around in a beautiful display of color over naked glistening bodies. They dropped the fabric, letting it float to the ground around them and ran their hands and lips over each other until all three were squirming on the ground. They suckled at breasts and thighs, hips pumped and thrust in lust and need.

The music pounded and moved quickly, matching the twisting and pulsing of the girls, one was twitching non-stop, moaning loudly, close to release. The girl at her core sucked harder and the one at her breast bared her teeth again on the nipple. She shuddered and screamed, long and lingering, unknowing or uncaring who watched at this point. The other two girls laid across her as they pleasured each other and soon they screamed in unison, a tangle of limbs and sweat and lust. The music dropped off then three steady beats rang out. The girls untangled themselves and moved slowly back to their places at the wall, now naked and spent, but kneeling and ready to serve again should it be desired.

"Very nice, Ielle-kyr," he said to her, giving an extra tug on the binding and watching her breath catch at the pull. Obin appeared to be enjoying it. He pulled his girl across his lap and was fondling her freely, pushing her robes up to her hips.

The rest of the evening went by in a blur. Kyr was finding it hard to concentrate for some reason. He spoke when needed, hearing his conversation as if it came from someone else. Ielle's fingers on his thigh were the only thing that seemed grounded and real.

It must be this damned plague within his house. It was consuming him. It ate at him to think that someone in his ranks, most likely someone in this very room would harm the house of Kyr of Janos. Before this began it had never seriously been in his mind that one of his men would not be loyal to him. He had known most of them since childhood, nearly all had generations of service to his ancestors. What man would throw that away? And for what? A small step up in rank with some other Hausa? And what Hausa would want to take such a man under him? A man that could plot to take down his Hausa would not hesitate to take down the next one.

Ielle was looking at him with concern in her eyes. He smiled at her and stroked her hair. His head was beginning to pound but it would not do to cut short the evening with his guest unless his condition was dire. It was not dire. Just annoying. He would have Ielle give him a massage with some healing oils later. Something about wrapping himself in her softness always made him feel better. Finally, the evening was drawing to a close. He could escape this endless prattle.

"Obin of Mashet, the house of Kyr of Janos would like to offer you Mayia-bylar to attend to your furs tonight, should it please you." He caught Obin's gaze at Ielle, but kept his own face neutral. Ielle was not on offer, hopefully it would not become an issue, but either way, it would not occur. Obin turned to look at Mayia, taking in her beauty. Excellent, he agreed to have her attend him. He should have a fine night with both girls working on him. Mayia rose from her place at Bylar's side, moving to kneel before Obin, sliding her hands up to cup her breasts and offer herself to him. She cuddled in beside him, smiling at the girl that was still draped across his knees.

Kyr snapped his fingers at one of the house girls, motioning for her to present herself to Bylar. All was well, everyone was attended to, there was no offense to anyone and now blessedly he could retire to his own furs.

He laid heavily upon the pallet, allowing Ielle to tend to him, enjoying the feeling of her gentle hands removing his clothing. He shifted and lifted to help her, but his head got heavier every minute. She begged him to lay back and allow her to massage him. It was easy to agree and even easier to lose himself to the sensations of her caresses on his skin. She knelt over him, providing him with a lovely view of her bouncing breasts and the knot rubbing against her while she massaged the oils into his chest. She moved around behind him, propping her own back against the wall and pillowing his head into her lap

127

so that she could flex her fingers into his shoulders and neck, gently massaging across his forehead and temples.

The next thing he knew it was morning. The headache was still there, but much lessened from the day before. Ielle was still under him, sleeping propped up against the wall, her hands resting lightly on his head. He smiled to himself. His beautiful girl. She would have watched over him the entire night, dozing from time to time when exhaustion could no longer be pushed back.

He slipped from the bed, leaning over to shift Ielle so that she could lay comfortably, covering her with the furs then leaving a kiss on her lips. He watched her a moment, smiling as she snuggled into the warmth and fell into a deeper sleep. He called Ama and let her know that Ielle was not be to disturbed. Perhaps he could get rid of this annoying headache today when he met with Obin's mystic.

Bringing together two mystics could often have powerful results. They had a way of magnifying each other's energy and creating additional clarity. The two mystics had spent the night together, chanting and meditating. They would be ready soon to tell him the results. In the meantime, he would have more tedious conversation with Obin about inconsequential matters. Thankfully Bylar would be there to carry much of the discussion for him.

"Good dawn to you, Obin," he said entering the meeting area and taking a seat. "I hope your sleep was pleasant and our girl was pleasing to you."

"Yes, yes, quite, thank you. She's quite nice in the furs, Bylar. You must enjoy her very much."

"I'm glad she was pleasing."

"She was quite entertaining. We had a little contest. I tied them together, head to tail and had them battle to see who would release first. Your girl had Bata screaming her head off, not just licking and sucking either, she was driving her tongue in there, taking her teeth to her. She left bruises on her ass from her fingers, nips on her thighs and a mark across her mound from sucking so hard. Bata didn't stand a chance."

"Then they both knelt beside me, taking turns licking their tongues over my hard cock. One stroke from Mayia, one from Bata, flicks from Mayia, kisses from Bata. Competing with each other to please me."

"I had them kneeling next to each other, going back and forth between their mouths, then later head down, asses high going back and forth between their holes. I quite enjoy having the two at once really. They're competitive little beasts. Each one vying to be the most pleasing. I'm happy to return the favor anytime to either of you. Bata is generally pleasing in the furs, but even more so when properly motivated."

Kyr really couldn't picture that happening any time soon but smiled and made the appropriate vague responses. He wouldn't rule out ever taking another girl alongside Ielle, but right now he didn't want to bother and definitely not with that kafai Bata.

It was some time later that the mystics announced they were ready to speak with him. They would have only him and Bylar in the session. Obin was not to come. He had not told Obin what the issue was. Although he doubted Obin would be part of a sophisticated plot, it was not wise to push that assumption at this point. The best feature about Obin was that he was such an ass. He had no skill at subterfuge or stealth. He would be an unlikely candidate to be part of the conspiracy. All he knew was that Kyr required an additional mystic to divine an issue. That was not an uncommon occurrence so there was no reason for suspicion on Obin's part.

Kyr and Bylar entered the mystic's chamber, finding it awash in colored incense. They settled on the furs, holding the divine crystals between them and concentrating on the issue at hand. Obin's mystic spoke up almost as soon as they were in position.

One who wishes you harm is in this house. Now. As we speak. The feeling is very strong. Resentment, jealousy. Hatred. Greed." Kyr was taken back a bit by the vehemence of the words spitting forth from the mystic. He thought it was interesting it was not related to power as he would have expected. Something much more personal clearly. "You must be on guard. Those that would help you are in danger. Those that would warn you are in danger. My apologies, Hausa, I do not have more. Just an intensity that is alarming."

"You have done well. The house of Kyr of Janos thanks you both for your work."

CHAPTER THIRTEEN
~ IELLE ~

Ielle awoke in the furs, snuggling into them for a minute then realizing that Kyr was gone. She called Ama and questioned her as to his condition this morning and was relieved to hear that he seemed fine. She hoped this situation with the spy would be resolved soon. She could see it weighing on him.

She soaked in the pools, letting her mind drift, then was re-wrapped into the blue rope. Kyr loved the way it looked on her. She loved the way it held her body, reminding her of his touch. Ielle suspected he particularly loved the way the knot rubbed on her, making her even more needy and desperate for him by the end of the day.

She attended to Obin's girls, ensuring they were

rested and had everything they needed. Bata required a lot of attention, much as Mayia did. She was constantly asking for this and that to be brought to her. As a hostess, Ielle was quick to accommodate, and had two house girls assigned to Bata's beck and call, but still she seemed to constantly come up with one thing after another. Ielle could not imagine doing the same if the positions were reversed. She would be a gracious guest and not impose.

She was stuck with the girls and the household matters. There was no respite since the men were occupied with their matters elsewhere. Bata's requests were tedious and wore on her as the day went on. Mayia stayed by Bata's side. They whispered together, clearly laughing at Ielle.

Pithai worm snakes. Ielle bit her tongue and decided not to squabble with them. Her most important charge was to ensure Kyr's happiness. He would not be happy if she should battle with the girls of his guest. Instead, she had treats and delicacies brought to them, hoping they would entertain themselves for a bit with the noon meal.

Word finally came that Obin's party would be leaving that afternoon, heading towards home so that they could make camp en-route before nightfall. It would be three days to get to their lands. They were far on the outskirts of territory friendly to the house of Janos.

Mayia and Bata embraced and giggled together, whispering quietly and sneaking looks at Ielle. It would be good riddance to the bad combination that occurred when the two came together.

Ielle felt a bit badly that she was relieved they were leaving. The burdens of their visit were heavy and it was good to know that she would not need to worry about them any longer. It was also a relief to know there would be no more concern about what Mayia might do to bring embarrassment to Kyr.

She lined the girls up in the courtyard to bid Obin's house safe journey. Each girl knelt in a line, heads bowed in deference to the guests. Kyr and his men spoke to Obin and his staff, the stable hands held the mareshi for them while they mounted. Provisions were lashed to the beasts, girls were handed up, generally sitting behind their owners.

Bylar would accompany them to their lands to ensure all went well with their travels. It was an extra precaution that was not explained, but Ielle knew it was due to the concern about the enemy within. She noticed Kyr speaking quietly and earnestly to Bylar before bidding everyone a merry farewell and much thanks.

Once the guests had left, Kyr returned to a series of meetings with advisors. Makir and two of the house guards kept very close to Kyr, never leaving him alone for a moment for the rest of the day. Ielle sent the girls to rest and relax and did the same herself, snuggling back into Kyr's furs for a nap. It was nearly time to line up in the alcove for the night meal when a house girl came running into the chamber.

"Ielle, Ielle, quickly, the master is ill!" She ran off, following the girl, her heart racing with concern. When she arrived, he was reclined, his eyes closed, his body bathed in sweat. He was shivering and could not speak coherently.

Makir and the house guards brought him to his chamber. He was settled in his furs, guards posted at his doors. She shooed the rest away and set about undressing him herself, reluctantly accepting help from Makir in order to get his clothing off.

Makir sent for the healer immediately, but in the meantime, she had Ama bring her cloths, a bowl of cool water and the healing oils. She massaged her hands over him, spreading the healing oils, knowing this was more than the ordinary occurrence, but knowing she had to try.

She bathed his forehead with cool cloths, tears welling in her eyes. He was breathing quietly, but he was breathing. He moaned from time to time and tossed restlessly, but did not fully wake.

Perhaps this was his plan. Yes, surely this must be it. He must have taken some potion that would mimic sickness in order to draw out the plot! She tried to hold to that hope, praying to the gods that he wasn't really as ill as he appeared.

The healer arrived in a swirl of ribbons and cloaks. He brushed one stroke each of six different potions across Kyr's chest, watching for any to change color. When one shifted from red to blue, he shook his head.

He spoke officially to Makir but Ielle was there to hear as well. There was a poison in his system. He would try some antidotes but he could not know for sure if they would work. It was difficult since the actual type of poison was not known. Kyr was to be kept quiet and resting, take fluids as much as he could. They were to bathe his skin to keep the fever down and pray for the best.

Makir took charge, sending the fastest stable hand on the fastest mount to bring Bylar back. They had a huge head start and mareshi did not usually ride at night, no matter how urgent the mission. It would take a day or more to reach him and then a few more for him to return. Additional guards were posted at the doors to Kyr's chambers and anyone bringing food or drink to the room would be required to taste it themselves before it would be allowed inside the door.

Kaiu came often, sitting with Ielle, praying with her to the gods for Kyr. Ielle sent her to rest, worried that she was becoming ill herself with the strain.

Of course Ielle would not leave his side. She spooned tiny bits of soup through his lips as often as she could. She held him against her under the furs when he shivered uncontrollably. She bathed his skin with cool wet cloths when he burned with fever.

She slept next to him each night, determined that no one else would get near to him. Makir stayed in the room as well, keeping an additional watch. He had ordered a search of the grounds in an attempt to find the poison, but so far he had not been able to uncover it.

They were both relieved when there was a pounding in the hall and Bylar came bursting through the door. He barreled across the floor to Kyr's side. Ielle gave him the report from the healer, showing Bylar what they had been doing for the last two days.

"You've done well Makir. You also Ielle. Attend Kyr. I will take charge of the search and get the healer back here. There must be more that can be done." Bylar stormed off, throwing orders in his wake to anyone and everyone. Soon the house was a bustle of activity, guards were busy going through every nook and corner. Girls scurried hither and yon in a flash of sheer silks. No one was resting, everyone had something to do.

Ielle slipped back into the furs with Kyr, holding him against her to keep him calm. He did not thrash when she wrapped herself around him. She could hear his heart beating and know that he was safe a bit longer. She wiped the tears from her eyes, determined to stay strong to care for him. It was good that Bylar was back, but she could not let her guard down now. She must stay the course until Kyr was completely well again.

She was slipping small spoonfuls of broth through Kyr's lips when she heard yelling. Loud, angry shouts, Bylar's deep voice, then Makir's younger one. She frowned, unwilling to have them disrupt Kyr with whatever their dispute might be. She could not imagine what could bring them to such bellowing at a time like this. She set the bowl down, walking quickly to the hallway and slipping out the door, closing it softly behind her.

"What is this?" It was not done for a girl to confront such men, but she would not have Kyr upset. "Take your battle elsewhere, the master is too ill for such things outside his door." She glared at them both, determined she would have her way on this. Makir was looking at her sadly and Bylar seemed to be looking everywhere but at her.

"What is the matter now? What is going on?"

Bylar nodded at the door guard and the next thing she knew he was grabbing her shoulders from behind while the other bound her hands.

"By the gods, Bylar, have you lost your mind? Kyr is ill, I must tend to him!" She struggled, trying to pull away but the guards were far too strong. Before she could think to kick her feet, they too were bound, then connected to the hands that were tied behind her. She lay on the floor, screaming and thrashing, but to no avail. Bylar actually stepped over her, entering Kyr's chamber and shutting the door behind him without a word.

"I'm sorry, Ielle," Makir said quietly, then instructed the guards to remove her.

CHAPTER FOURTEEN
~ KYR ~

His head was so heavy. He could not think. Something was very wrong. He was angry, troubled, anxious but unable to focus on anything specifically.

Someone was caring for him. Soft hands and limbs caressed him, gentled him. Cool cloths wiped his brow. Sips of water wet his lips and tongue. Ielle. Beautiful Ielle cared for him.

There were voices from time to time. Worried, concerned. Deep voices and soft feminine whispers. He could not capture the words, only the tone. Yes, something was very wrong.

It would be so easy to just slip away from this world, let it all rest behind him. Sleep, rest, slip away. What of Ielle if he died? She might pass as property to the new Hausa as a house girl. She might be sold to the rentals. No. No. He did not want that. He would fight for Ielle.

Gentle hands soothing him, whispers calming him. All would be well. Bylar would take charge. Makir would assist. The House of Kyr of Janos would not fall.

Where were the gentle hands? Ielle! Ielle! He must find her, she must be by his side. Strong deep voices, his men, his brothers. Yes, that is good. But where was Ielle? He must have Ielle.

Ah, she was back. Gentle hands on his brow again. He could rest, grow his strength to fight for Ielle.

CHAPTER FIFTEEN
~ IELLE ~

She lay on the floor and sobbed, her heart completely broken. She was sick with worry about Kyr and for some reason she was bound and shut up in a small cellar, away from him. It was dark, she could not gauge the time. She could not console herself, it was too much.

It was much, much later when the door slid open, hours and hours surely, days perhaps. The room was bathed by light from the adjoining hall. She blinked and would have shielded her eyes if she were not trussed into a bundle, unable to do more than squirm. Makir appeared with a house girl in tow. He set a torch in the holder in the wall and stood with his back against the door to guard that she would not escape. The house girl freed her wrists and feet, giving her a moment to flex and bend and restore the circulation.

"Makir, is Kyr all right? You must tell me, please." She crawled to him, bowing her head to his feet, desperate to know.

"He lives, Ielle. He is as you left him. Ama and Bylar attend him. The healer has been again and searches for an antidote to the poison."

"Thank the gods." She could barely speak she was so overcome with the knowledge that he still lived. "Makir, what has happened? Why am I here? Please."

"Patu, Ielle." She sucked back her sobs and leaned back on her heels, presenting her arms for binding in front. When she was bound he had the house girl bring in a bowl of broth, some bread and a thin blanket. The house girl took a sharp knife and cut the decorative blue ropes from her, leaving her naked. She was not even to have that symbol of Kyr's touch on her skin to sustain her. All that remained was Kyr's chain on her waist.

"Makir, please, I do not know why you treat me thus."

"We found the vial, Ielle."

"The poison? Thank the gods! Then the healer may make an antidote!"

"Yes, we hope so. That spoils your plan does it not?"

"What? What are you talking about?" She could hear her voice rising in panic, what did he mean?

"We found it where you hid it, Ielle, among your things. It was hidden well, but we found it before Kyr could breathe his last. You should be proud, we were taken in by you, nearly to the detriment of Kyr. Thank the gods we found you out before you could complete the plot. Did you mean him to linger long or were you planning to finish him soon with a second dose? Were you so unhappy you would prefer to become a house girl to the next Hausa?"

"Makir, I... I cannot even hear your words. I would never even imagine such a thing."

"No? Was it not your idea to have Kyr feign illness to draw out the enemy? Was it your plan to use that chance to sicken him in truth? Instead you acted when Bylar was away. Too bad for you the dose was not strong enough to act faster and you did not hide the evidence better."

"Makir... you do not know me better than that?"

"I thought I did, Ielle. It seems I do not."

"Makir-"

"No more, Ielle. You will stay here until the master recovers and can deal with you. If he does not..." Makir shrugged, his manner saying all that needed to be said should Kyr not survive.

They left, the torch still burning in the holder. Ielle curled up into the corner, huddled under the blanket, unable to stop shivering, although the room was not especially cold. She had no interest in the food, she had no interest in life if Kyr should not live. How could they think she would do such a thing to anyone? How could they think she could do such a thing to Kyr. She drifted to sleep, exhausted, only to wake with a start, dreaming of Kyr. She hoped that her imprisonment was a nightmare but it seemed too real for that hope to linger. She prayed devotedly for the gods to save him, for the healer to find the antidote, for it to reach him in time. Even if she should perish, she could not face that Kyr should not recover.

The torch burned out and she lay in the darkness. It seemed suitable, all was dark with her world. There was nothing, she was nothing without him. Eventually a guard came again and a house girl brought a new bowl of broth, the torch was replaced and they left without a word. She took a small sip to abate her thirst. It reached her empty belly and she felt it seep into her, feeding her. She sobbed anew, remembering all the times Kyr fed her at his side.

She finally slipped into a fitful sleep. She woke confused, unsure where she was for a moment then it all came rushing back. This time, she was able to push back the sorrow just a tiny bit. There was a small ember not yet snuffed deep in her soul. She was Ielle-kyr of Janos. Kyr needed her. She must survive to help him and she must think and work out who the real enemy was. If she should perish or if they were successful in blaming her, the real traitor would still be free to harm Kyr another time. They would not miss again she was sure.

With new resolve, she forced herself to finish the broth and choke down the stale bread. She would need strength to fight for Kyr. She could not give up and let them win. She pushed herself to her feet, her every muscle protesting. Slowly she paced her cage, a few steps each way, counting them out, willing her body and brain to begin working again. Over and over she moved, methodically considering everyone in the household, playing over every small word and deed.

Pangs of guilt plagued her for putting Kaiu, Bylar and Makir on her mental block for consideration as the traitor, but she knew it had to be done. She was relieved she could not find any reason to suspect them, but she would have to review them again if she should find no one else. Everyone was possible. She could not exclude anyone.

She heard footsteps in the hall and quickly slipped back to the floor. She would not let anyone know she was working on the puzzle. She would not tip the enemy.

The door opened and one of the guards entered, bringing a new torch. She looked up to see the house girl following him and gasped.

"Mayia! Why do you attend here? This does not seem your level of sport."

Mayia set the food down sloppily, not caring what spilled. "True. But I was interested to see the one that would harm her master. Much nerve you have, Ielle. I did not suspect it." She stepped closer to Ielle, leaning down to peer into her face. "You do not look like the property of the Hausa now, Ielle. Not so high and mighty are you?"

Ielle refused to let Mayia bait her. She must not betray her strength right now, must save what energy she had to help Kyr. She ignored the jibes, waiting for Mayia to get on with it and leave. "Haitu, Ielle." Mayia was grinning widely.

"You do not master me, Mayia."

"Perhaps not yet. I may ask Kyr to give you to me though. Assuming he lives. And if there's anything left of you by then. It would be fun to have you. You could service me. I would have you service all the men of the house, they would take you over and over. In every way imaginable. The high and mighty Ielle crawling through the household from man to man begging him to use her. It would be so much fun to watch." She poked a finger sharply into Ielle's rib, making her want to flinch. "But in the meantime, you are still of this house, so you do still bow to that do you not?" Mayia nodded to the guard.

"Haitu, Ielle," the guard said.

By the gods. She took a deep breath, drawing on her training, drawing on Kyr, determined not to shame him. She got awkwardly to her feet, standing solidly, spreading her legs the width of her shoulders. She bent double, her bound hands resting lightly on the floor between her feet, exposing herself to Mayia and the guard. She closed her eyes and waited. Mayia's glee radiated from her.

It took every fiber of her being not to flinch at the touch of Mayia's hand on her rear. She felt her stroking over the skin, poking at the dark pucker. She bit her lip when Mayia pinched a lower lip hard, twisting and digging in with her fingers.

"When Kyr gives you to me, I'll have you like this every day, Ielle. This is how you will stand before me when you are in my presence." She slapped hard at Ielle's rear, nearly knocking her over with the force. Ielle fought back the cry that was at her lips, determined not to feed Mayia's fever.

"Shaiku, Ielle," the guard called out. She shuddered but slipped to her back, the stinging remnant of Mayia's hand on her backside rubbing against the hard ground. She pressed the bottoms of her feet together, pulling her knees up and open. She could not properly finger her nipples with her hands bound, but completed the position as best she could. Mayia stood over her, sneering. Ielle could see why people thought Mayia beautiful, but all she could see right now was the ugliness that wrapped around her.

"You cannot complete the position can you? I shall show a kindness and help you then." Mayia reached into her robes and pulled out some of those wicked wooden clamps. Ielle stared at her with defiance, determined to keep her head about her no matter what. She drew in air, steeling herself but even so, she gasped at the bite when they were screwed down impossibly tight.

"I would have you like this too. For hours every day. Pinching your nipples, rolling them in your own hands at my order. Your core wide open for whatever I choose to insert, your mouth open to suck whatever I choose to have you suck. Yes, it would be glorious would it not?"

Ielle bit off a scream when Mayia's hand came down hard on the tender skin of her thighs. Over and over she slapped, the noise echoing off the walls, tears leaking from Ielle's eyes.

"I would punish you like this every day too, but I would not use my hand. Perhaps a switch or a strap. Maybe both." She stopped, then abruptly yanked the clamps from Ielle's breasts. White hot pain spiraled through her but she held the position. She would not shame Kyr, even if he should never know or care again.

Mayia flounced to the door, then ran back and

gave her a solid kick in the side. Ielle curled up in pain, hearing the door close behind them. She rocked herself, holding her side, knowing there would soon be a huge bruise. She inched her fingers to pull the blanket over herself, saving her strength for the battle for Kyr.

CHAPTER SIXTEEN
~ KYR ~

The weight on his head lifted a bit. Soft hands were there to stroke and massage him, working at his brow, rubbing across his chest with the fresh scent of healing oils. Ah, Ielle. He clumsily moved his hand to touch her, unable to fully focus, but a little better able to reach reality than before. She took his hand in hers, whispering gently until he slept again.

He woke later, much more awake this time. She was curled against him. He tangled his fingers in her hair, wanting to feel her, rubbing the strands between his fingers. The lights were low, it was not quite black in the room but very dark. He played with the lock of hair. Wait. This was not right. He struggled to sit up, unable to push himself off the furs, but trying none the less. She woke, stroking his chest softly, shhhh... gentling him. He flopped back down, trying to make sense. No. Not right.

"Ielle." His voice was hoarse, his throat parched and dry.

"Shhh... All is well, you are safe and cared for, Master." No, it was wrong. Not Ielle. Someone else. He shoved her with all the strength he had. It was not much he knew, he was very weak, but it was enough to knock her from his side.

"Shhh... rest, Kyr, all is well." Bylar. Yes, that was right. That was the weight of Bylar's hands on his shoulders, settling him down.

"Ielle."

"Ama is here for you, Kyr. She nurses you."

"Ielle." He struggled to make it a command not a question. He wanted Ielle. No other girl would do.

"She rests, Kyr. She will return later. Ama cares for you until then." He relaxed. This was good. Bylar would care for Ielle.

The next time he stirred there was a foul smell at his nose and an odd taste at his lips. He absently brushed it away, then realized he could barely lift his hand.

"A healing potion, Kyr." Bylar again. Good. "It draws the sickness from you and builds your strength. You are much better now. We were quite worried for some time."

He parted his lips in an effort to help. The liquid slipped into his mouth and down his throat. It was terrible, but if it would clear his head, he would take it. He thought he heard Bylar and Makir talking but could not quite make out the words. Enemy. Plot. Ah yes, that was it. The sickness must have to do with that. It was too much to puzzle out now, but he would put his mind to it later.

He woke and slept, taking in the foul healing elixir, trying to build his strength. He became aware of a nourishing broth being fed to him, he did not need to waste energy to chew. Each time he woke it seemed his mind worked a bit better.

Finally he roused, exhausted but clear. He slowly wiggled his fingers and toes and although they were weak, they responded properly to his command. He moved to flexing his knees. Yes, it was hard to do, but they moved and responded. The room was dark but he knew he would not be alone. He levered himself up, a grunt and a moan slipping from him at the effort but he succeeded, sitting upright for the first time in who knew how long. Thankfully, his head remained clear. The pounding was gone. Finally, finally, gone.

"Bylar!" He called out, hearing it come out much more softly than he expected. It was enough. Bylar popped up from a pallet nearby, instantly at his side, Ama grabbing pillows and fashioning herself behind him so that he could lean back against her. Good girl. He rested his weight heavily upon her. It was good to sit up though.

Bylar brought him a cup of cool water. The liquid slid down his parched throat, soothing the roughness. Ama reached around and helped him to hold the cup, ensuring it would not spill or fall. When he was done, she set it aside and massaged healing oils into his back while he talked with Bylar.

"Tell me, my friend. What has gone on? How long have I lain ill? Where is Ielle?"

Bylar took a deep breath, releasing it in a sigh. "It is twelve days, Kyr. You were poisoned. In your food we believe. You fell ill several hours after Obin left. Makir took charge and sent for the healer and to bring me back. He did you proud, Kyr."

Kyr nodded gently, not quite willing to tempt fate and move too quickly. "Go on. What of Ielle? Why is she not here?"

Again the sigh, the sadness in his eyes. "We made a search for the poison, several in fact. We found it finally. That gave the healer the ability to create the antidote."

Kyr wearily waved his hand. "Yes, get to the point. Where is Ielle?" His voice was getting loud now. Clearly there was something Bylar did not want to say. "Is she dead? Did she perish from the poison too?" His emotions rose up inside him, panic at the thought that Ielle might be gone. He knew she would be here if there was any way to make it happen.

"No, no, Kyr, she is not dead, she is not ill." Bylar laid his hand on Kyr's. "But you're right, there is more. We found the vial of poison among her things, Kyr. It was well hidden. It did not come to light during the first few searches, it took great stealth to find it."

He slumped his full weight against Ama as though he had been kicked by a mareshi. "By the gods, Bylar. It cannot be."

"We believe it to be so, Kyr. She was caring for you, playing the part, pretending concern for your illness. All the while she was the enemy, either enjoying making you linger or hoping to finish you off with a final dose at some point. We have her secured, you can deal with her when you are better."

His stomach dropped and he fought back nausea. "I must rest now, Bylar, my friend and brother. I thank you all for your service during this time."

"We are here, Kyr, by your side." Bylar helped Ama to lay Kyr back down. He was spent. It was too much to hear. His heart was not broken, it was shattered into a thousand pieces. It could never be repaired. Was there any chance there was a mistake? He hoped so, but it seemed unlikely. Bylar was excellent at his job, he would have been thorough and sure before he took action.

Ama crept under the covers and cuddled herself against him, but he nudged her away. She meant to keep him warm and help him heal, but he could not stand the soft feminine touch right now. Ielle. He drifted into a blessed dreamless blackness.

Over the next few days he struggled to regain his strength. He pushed himself harder than Bylar would like. It exhausted him, but it was crucial for a Hausa to lead. He must return to his place as soon as possible. He must let his enemies know that the house of Kyr of Janos was solid and stable. It also pushed thoughts of Ielle from his head. He knew he would need to deal with her at some point, but he must have all his strength back first. At least on the outside. He was not sure he would ever have the same inner strength again but he could not let them know that.

Ummi visited him daily, hugging him tightly, kissing his cheeks. Several times he caught her secretly trying to wipe tears from her eyes, still feeling the near loss of her son. He made sure that her chamber maid kept a close eye on her. He was worried that the strain of his illness was too much for her. He ordered her to rest and relax, take to the pools, eat well. She smiled and nodded and told him not to fuss, but they both knew she was not taking care of herself.

He stood much before they wanted him to, taking shaky steps around his chambers, leaning heavily on Makir. He dressed himself. Not well, truth be told, but he waved them away when they would try to help. He forced down the potions and elixirs they pushed on him and choked down the stews and foods, knowing he needed the strength in his limbs. Soon he could manage to make his way around his house, even though he leaned heavily on a stout walking stick.

Finally, he knew he could avoid it no longer. He must deal with Ielle, still locked up in a cellar room. He resolved to see her the next morning and begin deciding her fate. It was like a sword through his heart, but his duty as a Hausa and an owner was clear.

Ummi entered, crossing the floor to his feet, settling beside his furs. She was one of the few allowed in his chambers. He still had extra guards and he would never again take food or drink that was not tested first. It was a loss to him to know that he must do so in his own home. If he could not trust Ielle, how could he trust anyone?

"Good evening to you, Ummi. Your son is nearly well, see?" He wiggled his toes at her, hoping to make her laugh and forget her worries. She smiled at him, but it was weak. The light did not reach her eyes.

"Kyr, I am so glad you are nearly well. I must ask you now though..." She took his hand in hers and patted it gently. "Kyr, is it true? What they say about Ielle? Can it be?"

Again, the kick to his stomach. Would there ever be a time when he could even think of her and her betrayal? He swallowed hard, pushing back the bile that rose.

"It seems so, Ummi. The poison was found among her things. Well hidden. She talked to me of poison and plots, sneaking and scheming. She is bright, she could do it easily. She..." He took a deep breath, struggling to go on. "She had my trust, Ummi. She was the one who could make it happen over anyone else."

A tear dropped from Ummi's eye, landing briefly on his hand before she brushed it away with her own. "My son, you are good to your mother. Would you grant her something very important to her? A symbol of a son's affection?"

By the gods, she was to ask of him something huge. He hoped he could grant it. "May I hear what it is first, Ummi, or must I be blind in my devotion?"

She wiped her eyes then took his hand in hers again. "Kyr, will you not rush to condemn Ielle? Will you bring back the mystic of Obin, or another perhaps, first? See if they may know anything?" He knew doubt showed on his face, she looked at him pleadingly. She had never asked him for anything before. She did not ask him to pardon the girl or to show mercy in the punishment, only to be sure first.

"Why do you ask this, Ummi?"

"Kyr, I am old. I have lived a long time and I like to think I have seen much of life. I see the women when you do not. I see them in the pools, at their leisure, when they might gossip and be kuckai, when they might be kind and no one knows. I have seen Ielle and I believe I have seen her heart, and her heart for you. She does not benefit from this move. At best she would be assigned as a house girl to Bylar if you had died. That might be fine for a girl that hates her master, but I did not see that with Ielle. Why should she want that? She has only ever wanted you."

"I saw her caring for you, tears in her eyes hour after hour. Her ear on your chest to ensure your heart would still beat. Taking no rest or food of her own, bathing you, warming you, holding you, praying for you. Terrified, yet showing strength for you. I could be wrong, Kyr. I could be. But it does not seem that is the heart of your enemy."

She kissed his hand, holding him warmly in her palm. "Please, Kyr. Please be sure." He gently cupped her cheek, rubbing his thumb along her jaw as she used to do when he was a young boy and needed comfort. Her eyes were pained, she cared so much for Ielle. She had embraced her as a daughter. It was possible neither of them could see her clearly now. She was wise, his Ummi. And formidable. She would not let this go without sharing her thoughts on it first, even if it made him unhappy with her. It was a great gift for her to give to Ielle, a risk she took on Ielle's behalf. The least he could do is honor his Ummi and grant her request.

CHAPTER SEVENTEEN
~ IELLE ~

She wasn't sure if food came daily or not. It might be only every two or three. She could not tell since there was no day or night. She still did not really want it, but she took it anyway, knowing she needed to do her best to care for Kyr's property if there was any hope to help him. At least as long as she stayed here, she could know he still lived. She did not think they would let her linger long if he died.

Mayia came again. Ielle was still in pain from the last visit and stayed curled up in the corner, hoping she would go away.

"Bartu, Ielle," the guard said.

She sighed, knowing this was not going to be easy. She pushed up to her knees, head down, legs spread, leaning heavily on her bound hands.

"We should warm her ass first, should we not?" Mayia addressed the guard, cuddling up to him and stroking her hands over his chest. He grinned at her and nodded. She grabbed between his legs, making him catch his breath.

Ielle steeled herself, closing her eyes. Something hard and flat landed across her rear. A sandal, it seemed. Over and over until finally she was whimpering in spite of herself. She bit her lip, holding back, but could not stop the tears that spilled forth. Damn that kuckai, Mayia.

The spanking stopped and Ielle held still, waiting to see what Mayia would do next. Of course there will be something else. She flinched when the finger entered her.

"See how she is? Come, have a feel." The guard laughed and obliged, roughly shoving his own finger into Ielle.

"They'll put all kinds of things in here at the rentals, girl," he said. "It will be a grand day if it is only a finger or two, and only in this hole instead of another." Ielle chewed on her lip, trying to pretend this was not happening. He wiped his damp finger over her burning rear, then stood.

"Hurry up, Mayia. I've got to get back to my post soon and you know we have things to do first."

"Yes, and you know how much you're going to

enjoy doing them, aren't you?" Mayia was rubbing herself against the guard. "Just one more thing."

Ielle screamed at the savage kick to the same spot in her ribs. She rolled to the ground, curled up in a ball. She was sure the bone had broken, it was painful to get even a shallow breath.

She did not know how much later she woke. She was in a lot of pain, the cold stone floor and thin blanket making her aches worse. Still this was better than she could expect if they should believe she had done this thing to Kyr. If she lived, at best she could end up a house girl, maybe to Mayia. More likely sold to the rentals after a punishment. Rental girls were beaten regularly by many owners and customers. They begged their customers to feed them and languished when they did not. She'd be lucky to be in the shape she was now after a few days with them. Shivers ran over her skin and she pushed the ugly thoughts away. She must focus on the here and now.

Days were surely passing, but again, she couldn't tell how many. She could barely eat when more food came. She had to drag herself to wherever the bowl was left. She was unable to pace her cage while she thought, her ribs far too sore to let her stand on her own with her hands tied as they were. Still, she worked her brain over every word and deed of every member of the house, filing away anything she thought might at some point add up.

The door scraped open and blinding light filled the dark room. She covered her eyes then blinked. Kyr! By the gods, it was Kyr! He was weak, he leaned heavily on a walking stick, he was flanked by Bylar and Makir, but it was Kyr. She burst into tears of joy, dragging herself to his feet, bowing her head, her bare ass high before him, sobbing with happiness.

"Up, Ielle." He nudged her shoulder roughly with his foot. His voice was hoarse and full of emotion. She moved as quickly as she could, struggling, wincing, unable to get fully upright. Makir reached down and hauled her abruptly to her feet while she cried out in pain. She stood before him, her bound hands settled under her breasts as was proper. She saw the shock in his eyes, she was sure she must be a sorry sight. Still she could not hide her delight in seeing him alive and so much better.

He stepped forward and traced a finger over her side, following the outline of the large angry bruise. She thought she might never again have his touch on her skin. Even his light hand brought new pain to the area, but she did not care, it was Kyr, he was alive and he was here.

"What happened to you?"

"It is not important. I am nothing. I am so happy to see you so well, Kyr." She was shocked when a slap landed across her cheek. It was all she could do not to bring her hands to it but she held the position.

Tears welled in her eyes. It was a sound blow, although it did not bring blood and could have been worse. The greater blow was his displeasure. She knew to expect it, knew they thought her a traitor, but it was still stunning to have it in front of her.

"You will answer what I ask. I decide what is important. You are still my property, I control my house."

"Yes, Master," she said quietly, casting her eyes down and trying to blink back the tears and absorb the sting.

"I ask again. What happened to you?"

"It is from a kick, Master. Two actually."

"From my men?"

"No, Master, from a girl who attended me." Her chest worked harder and harder to breathe, her words getting softer since she could not get a full breath. She was dizzy, it was hard to think now.

"Which of my house girls takes it on herself to discipline my property?" He was thundering now. He may hate her, but he would not have the rest of his house out of control either.

She opened her mouth to answer and felt the room pitch. She slumped to the floor, collapsing into a puddle, unable to speak or breathe, dissolving into blackness.

~

Pain. Relax, submit, find harmony. Or at least reduce misery. She made an effort to comply but it did not help much. She had shooting pain in her side and a stinging burn over her face from his slap. She moved to rub her hand on her cheek and discovered she was bound to a pallet of furs, her arms stretched to each side. She was inclined, nearly sitting upright, her breathing easier than it had been for days. She shifted, realizing her ankles were bound too. She was not uncomfortably tied, but she would not be going anywhere anytime soon.

"Shhh... Rest, Ielle," a soft voice spoke near her ear. She opened her eyes and turned her head.

"Kaiu! Why do you attend me?"

"Shhh... You are in my chambers, Ielle. The healer has seen to you and you shall remain under my care until Kyr decides what to do about you."

Once again, tears spilled from her eyes. Kaiu rested a cool cloth on Ielle's cheek, easing the pain there.

"Oh, Kaiu." She sighed. Was there any hope for her?

"Ielle," Kaiu spoke in a serious tone, searching her eyes carefully. "I have loved you as a daughter. You have been a blessing to my son and shown every kindness and respect to me. I have only ever begged Kyr for two indulgences. Both for you and both in one day. Please, please, honor me a final time with the truth. If you did this thing, say so now and we will not speak of it again. I will ensure you are treated humanely until the judgment is made. But please, Ielle, tell me honestly, I beg of you, Ielle. Tell this old woman that she does not err when she says she sees your true heart and devotion to her son." Ielle blinked back her own tears, watching Kaiu's fall.

"Please, Kaiu. I could never even think such thoughts. May the gods take me now. You do know my heart, Kaiu." They locked eyes. It was a long deep look between them. Finally a nod.

"Yes, Ielle. I do know your heart and your character. I am glad I have begged on your behalf today." Ielle did not realize she had been holding her breath for the verdict until she released it in a whoosh. She grimaced at the pain that caused, noticing for the first time the healing plaster and binding on her torso. Kaiu followed her gaze. "You had two broken ribs, girl. Who did this? Kyr has had every house girl who served you lined up but none has yet confessed."

"That kafai, Mayia. She came twice just to torment me."

Kaiu nodded. "How did she manage that?"

"I do not know, but both times she was with that young light-haired guard. The thin one with the blue eyes."

"Yes, yes, I know of which you speak. I will pass

that to Kyr. He is furious. Of course it is obvious he will not have his property damaged or his authority usurped. But as a mother, I know. His heart hurts to see you so, Ielle."

"Kaiu, is he well? Really?"

"Yes. He is recovering nicely, pushing too hard, doing too much. Stubborn like his father." She could not help but smile softly at the thought. "Physically, he will be well. But his heart is shattered. If we cannot show that you are innocent of this crime and who truly does this thing... I fear it will never mend."

More tears slipped from her eyes. Would she never stop crying?

"Kaiu, what can we do? More important than my fate, someone in this house wishes Kyr dead. He must be guarded closely. He can trust no one. They will not miss again. We must convince him."

"Shhh..." Kaiu stroked her shoulder gently. "He is safe for now, I promise. And I have convinced him to bring back Obin's mystic to help divine the truth. Until then, he is closely guarded by Bylar and Makir. He is served only by Ama and me. Likewise there is a guard at my door. No one but my chamber maid or I will attend you, Ielle. You will not be further abused until the judgment is resolved."

"Thank you, Kaiu. Whatever happens, please, if I cannot, promise me you will care for Kyr."

"Shhh, my girl. Rest. The healer has given you a

potion to help you sleep. We will talk more tomorrow when you are stronger and see what we can do to flush out the real enemy."

CHAPTER EIGHTEEN
~ KYR ~

Kyr sighed and rubbed his hand over his brow. He was getting nowhere with these house girls. One of them had abused his property. They had been lined up before him for over an hour, standing naked in haitu. Bent over with their legs spread, their calves must be burning, their heads must be swimming, backs would be aching. He did not care. He was nearly out of patience. They would crack soon or he would get serious about punishment for all. Ummi entered, slipping softly to his side, taking his hand in hers.

"Kyr, might I speak?"

He turned to her. His poor Ummi. This was so hard on her. Her eyes were red rimmed, she had cried a thousand tears over him, over Ielle, over all of it. He sent for Obin's mystic and he allowed her to care for Ielle. By the gods, let her not have yet another request. He didn't know if he was up to it and he did not think he could turn her down either.

"Yes, my Ummi."

"Ielle sleeps, but she stirred for a while. Her damage comes from Mayia."

"Mayia? How did she enter?"

"She did not know, but she came two times with the same guard. The thin, young, fair-haired one."

"Bylar!" Kyr felt his anger overflow. He clapped his hands and dismissed the girls. They scurried off quickly, faces red, heads probably spinning. He did not care.

Bylar entered from just outside the door. "Yes, Kyr, what is it?"

"Get that kuckai Mayia up here. And the guard. Varlir. Yes, that's his name. Both of them. Now."

"Yes, Kyr. Immediately." Bylar looked flustered and confused. Even for his brethren Bylar he did not care. All he could feel right now was wrath. He took deep breaths, attempting to control himself. He must be careful of his energy, he did not have full strength and he could not afford a relapse.

Bylar entered with his hand on Mayia's arm, pulling her along. Varlir came right behind, another guard escorting him.

"Naku, Mayia," Kyr said sharply. She hesitated. Of course. She glanced to Bylar. Of course. He pushed himself to his feet and took a step towards her. A sharp slap landed on her face, much harder than the one that he had given Ielle that morning. She cried out, falling to her knees, weeping and carrying on. Bylar wisely took a step back from her, distancing himself from whatever was going on.

"I am no longer playing with you, girl. Get on your feet and naku. Now. Do not look to Bylar. He may be your owner, but I am your Hausa."

At least the girl had the good sense to realize he was serious. She scrambled up and dropped her robes quickly, clasping her fingers together and settling her arms under her breasts. Her lip was swollen, her cheek bright red. She whimpered and tears fell from her like a waterfall. He did not care.

"Bylar, get a strap. I have questions for your girl and I do not have the patience for her anymore." Almost magically, one appeared in Bylar's hand, provided by the second guard.

"We begin. A strap across her ass first, Bylar. I wish her to be clear I do not toy today." Kyr settled himself back into his seat, giving Ummi's hand a pat while Bylar brought a solid stroke across the width of her ass, low on the cheeks, catching the most sensitive part, making her bellow and more tears stream from her eyes. Good. Bylar was not playing today either.

ANDRÉ SANTHOMAS

"Did you abuse my property, Mayia?" Again, she hesitated, her face working through all the possible answers she might give. A raised brow to Bylar and the strap slashed even harder over the top of her thighs. She screamed, loud and long.

"Shut up. I have no interest in your whining. Answer the question or get another. It is a simple thing." He nodded to Bylar and two more were delivered quick and hard, right on top of the last.

This time she contained herself better, but danced and stamped her feet. Bylar's arm was raised for another stroke when she cried out "Yes, yes, Master, yes. I did, Master, I beg forgiveness."

"Kyr, my brother, my apologies for my property. I had no idea." Bylar's face ran the gamut of shock, anger and embarrassment. He brought two more strokes across her rear even as he spoke to Kyr, her wail now high pitched and frantic. She dropped in a ball at his feet. "There will be a discard of course. I would be honored if you will attend with me when you are ready."

Kyr waved away the apology. He did not blame Bylar. "Of course. Once these other matters are settled we will tend to it."

"Shall I remove her now, my Hausa?"

"Not yet. There is more to this puzzle. Varlir, present yourself." Varlir seemed surprised. He should not be. He was there when it happened. He

176

shirked his duty to protect the property of his Hausa. He must know how angry his Hausa was over this. Varlir sunk heavily to his knees before Kyr, bowing his head.

"Did you allow this kuckai to abuse my property?"

"Yes, my Hausa."

"Explain yourself." He clenched and unclenched his fingers, attempting to calm down. Ummi's hand on his arm helped remind him to pace himself.

"Forgive my lapse, Hausa. I was not seeing her as your property, only as the evil enemy of your house. I did not take care of what she did to the girl. My Hausa, please excuse my youth and ignorance. I should have known better. If you will allow it, I shall withdraw from your service and return to my family's lands."

"Agreed." Varlir made to rise but Kyr held up a hand. "Wait. What did the kuckai do to entice you to bring her along?"

Varlir turned bright red and ducked his head in embarrassment. "She offered kammu, Hausa."

Kyr burst out laughing. "You risked my wrath over kammu? What magic does her mouth hold? Was she worth it? There are a dozen house girls you may have during your regular ration, any way you wish. You could ask for the service of this girl and probably get permission from her owner. Yet you throw away your honor over the forbidden encounter with a sulky spoiled girl?"

Bylar took a breath, then spoke. "My Hausa, please forgive him. It is the foolishness of youth. He has made a poor choice, as have many men over time. I believe he has learned from this one."

Kyr watched Bylar talk. He knew his friend was hurting, kicking himself for bringing such a girl into Kyr's household, not thinking things through to this conclusion. Truth be told, Kyr had not considered this particular outcome either, but he did know that one day there would be something along these lines. Bylar was watching him closely. They had grown up together, cousins as close as brothers. They had gotten into many scrapes and adventures together, plaguing their parents. He took his own deep breath. Yes, he could remember that foolishness of youth.

"Agreed. Varlir, return to your family lands. There will be no formal censure. I trust you will grow great wisdom from this encounter and that it will serve you well one day. You may go now."

"Thank you, my Hausa." He quickly rose and was escorted out by the second guard. Kyr relaxed a bit, some of his wrath dissipating.

Bylar was seething though, looking at Mayia, crumpled on the floor at his feet still sobbing and carrying on.

"I do not trust myself to even beat you, Mayia. If

I do it as I feel right now, there won't be enough of you left to make any coin from your sale. You embarrass yourself and your owner, bring disgrace to the house of Kyr of Janos, abuse his property and who knows what else, but then you must take down a good man in the process? And you've been shaking your ass to get what you want? You should hope you have skill in that area, Mayia. I'm told that those that take it up the ass the best get fed the most often at the rentals."

Mayia seemed to finally realize that she would not be wiggling out of her fate. Her face got deathly pale and for once, she shut up completely.

"Kyr, if you should approve, I have a use for her until the discard. Since she is so happy to offer her services to your staff, I shall establish her in the cellar room and let all the men know she is there for use until further notice. I'll leave the straps and whips and the clamps and the stone phallus of course. I'm sure some will find some very creative uses for such things."

"A fine idea my friend. But we should not forget the women may want to play too. Let them know they may visit if they have no other duties to attend to." Mayia looked absolutely petrified now. Good. She should be. He was sure the women would take out their revenge on her in some vicious ways. He did not care.

"She may go there now and begin. It will be good practice for her next career at the rentals." He was exhausted, his anger no longer holding him up. Ummi motioned to Bylar who handed Mayia over to another guard and came quickly to attend to Kyr.

He hated how heavily he had to lean on Bylar to retreat to his furs. By the gods, he did not even care of this girl or this guard. What would it take from him if he must do the same with Ielle? He settled back, taking the potions and elixirs from Bylar and Ummi. If nothing else, they would help him sleep and numb the pain in his heart.

CHAPTER NINETEEN
~ IELLE ~

Ielle woke to Kaiu's gentle hands on her side, check-ing the binding. She came fully awake realizing the healer was also there and they were discussing the plaster that was being used to bring down the bruis-ing and swelling.

Kaiu called the guard in to release the bindings on her arms and legs for a bit and give her a chance to stretch. The movement only served to remind her how really sore she was. She struggled to contain a moan of pain. She was so grateful to Kaiu for pleading to Kyr on her behalf. She might actually be dead by now if she were still on the floor of the cellar, and who knows if Mayia might have returned to finish her off. Of course if they couldn't prove her innocence, it might have been the best course in the long run, but she tried to push that from her thoughts.

"You're a fortunate girl," the healer said, packing up his tools. "You could easily have punctured a lung. This is quite a serious injury and it will take some time to fully heal."

Once he was gone, Kaiu settled down beside her, bathing her with a warm cloth. "The guard must bind you again now, but then we will talk alone." Ielle nodded, knowing she could not remain loose if the guard was not present. Even if she was not in the condition to rise on her own, they could not take the chance. She was accused of attempting to murder the Hausa. They would not take risks.

Once she was settled again and the guard had gone, she was able to speak freely. "Kaiu, tell me, is Kyr still well?"

Kaiu sighed. "He did too much yesterday. But he is fine, resting today. The healer has made him promise to spend the day in his furs and given him several more concoctions to improve his strength. He's not happy about it, but he knows the truth of it, so he rests."

Ielle nodded, picturing him there, probably propped up in his furs still conducting business and issuing commands even though he claimed to rest. She wished she could be by his side, helping him recover but it was not to be.

"So, I must tell you what it was Kyr was doing all day yesterday, my dear!" Kaiu settled in to relate the story of Mayia's interview before Kyr. Ielle shuddered as she heard it, knowing how furious he would have been. She couldn't imagine being the recipient of that rage, although she feared she may yet be in that position. She had a small twinge of sorrow for Mayia. She would be huddled on the same floor that Ielle had so recently laid on, but in addition, she would be used and abused by all and sundry. By the gods. Ielle might have the same fate any time now too. At least Mayia deserved hers though, terrible as it was. She had only brought it upon herself.

"It should be some small solace to you that she does not get away with this act against Kyr's property, Ielle."

"Yes, thank you for telling me, Kaiu. It is a shame she did not do better. Bylar must be very upset. How does he fare?"

"He is quite distraught although he tries not to show it. I have known him forever, so I see it. But Kyr will attend the discard with him when he is better. All is well between them. Men are fortunate that way. They live as brothers and get over their spats quickly. Women tend to sulk and scheme and look for any further slight to bolster their case."

Ielle nodded, knowing that was true so often. She looked deeply into Kaiu's face, noting the red rims of her eyes, the lines that had deepened over the brow. "Kaiu, you do too much. You are caring for Kyr, you are caring for me. Please, you must keep well. If not for yourself then for Kyr. He will need you when I am gone."

"Shhh... Do not think like that, Ielle." Kaiu brought her a bowl of hearty stew and fed her while they talked. "I am tougher than I look. I will rest properly when this is all behind us. Until then, I am fine, I promise my girl." Ielle pretended to believe her, knowing she was far from fine, but unable to do anything about it as things stood. She prayed that if things should somehow work out, she would be able to care for Kaiu one day to repay her just a small bit for her kindness.

~

Over the next two days, Kaiu and Ielle spent many hours talking and thinking and praying for an answer. When she was not attending Ielle, Kaiu was at Kyr's side. He was behaving himself at least, staying in his chamber and saving his energy. That was one small worry off the minds of both Ielle and Kaiu.

Obin arrived, once again bringing his mystic and men and their girls. Kaiu did not serve them, she was too busy with Kyr and Ielle. Instead the hostessing fell to the stable master's girl. From the tales that

Kaiu shared, Obin's girl was still the same. Even the living example of the tortured Mayia did not dampen her. There would be a session tomorrow that Ielle was to attend.

The next morning she was prepared. The guard released her bindings and they helped her to sit up. The healer gave her a potion to reduce the pain. It was bearable, but still severe. Before she left the chamber, her hands were tied behind her back. Two guards helped her to move slowly through the hallways to the room where the session would happen.

She was hunched over when she entered, grateful when they allowed her to sink to her knees. Kaiu knelt beside her and a guard stayed right behind. A few feet away, Kyr, Bylar and Makir sat on furs. The circle was completed by the two mystics, their sacred rugs and billowing colored incense spilling forth. Lining the walls were all the girls and men of the house of Kyr of Janos. Girls knelt, men stood. Ielle noticed the surroundings, but really had eyes for no one but Kyr. If this day did not go well, this would be one of the last times she would be in his presence.

She could see he was worn and weary. Much better than when she attended him, true, but still a long way from the healthy man he was before he was stricken. He locked eyes with her and held her gaze a moment, bringing tears to her eyes. There was nothing but sorrow and pain. She didn't even find anger.

Kaiu moved a bit closer to her and wrapped an arm around her, pulling her in so that she could take physical and mental strength from her. What a blessing this woman was.

"Please, begin," Kyr said, nodding to the mystics. They rose, their ribbons and robes flowing around them as they sprinkled drops of various liquids into a brazier, watching the colors of the steam. They conferred in whispers.

"Hausa, there is a malevolent will within your walls." Ielle slumped a bit more against Kaiu. Yes, she certainly knew that to be the truth, but it was startling to hear it said so bluntly and by men with mystical sight.

"We wish to feel the energy of those that attend here. May we have your permission to do so?"

Kyr nodded. Ielle noticed several people shifted nervously. No one knew what form the test would take or what they would be looking for. She understood how even good people might be somewhat apprehensive.

One mystic pulled two clear crystals from a sack, holding them over the incense and saying a quiet prayer. The other filled a bowl with some small seeds of some kind. They stopped before Kyr, handing him the crystals and feeding him one of the seeds on the tip of his tongue. He was to hold the rocks out to the side, then bring them together in front of his chest.

Kyr watched the crystals converge in front of him. As soon as they touched, Ielle could see that the bases now had a distinctly gray cast to them.

"As expected, Hausa. That represents your illness and the strife you have recently endured."

The mystics moved to Bylar and then to Makir, each with a similar result. All various shades of gray. It was Kaiu's turn. Her gray was as dark as Kyr's. Ielle's hands were freed that she might participate also. Again, a deep gray.

They moved methodically along the wall. A seed and the crystals presented to each in turn. Lighter grays, often streaked with blues and greens. It seemed all carried some sorrow and concern for Kyr and the situation within the house of Kyr of Janos. When they finished with the last person, the mystics returned to the incense and consulted together.

"Hausa, there is no ill will towards you or your house within this room. This is however, still a great evil within your walls."

"How can that be?" Kyr turned to Bylar. "Who does not attend here?"

"No one, Kyr. All are present. The only others are of the house of Obin of Mashet."

Kyr shook his head in confusion then made up his mind. "Bring them. Please let Obin know it is to be considered a favor to our house that he attend." Bylar hurried off with two of the guards. "I shall be indebted to Obin for this. Please pray this is worth our while," Kyr said to the mystics.

Obin, his men and girls filled in a few minutes later. The mystics refreshed the crystals and the bowl. Kyr addressed them.

"Obin, the house of Kyr of Janos thanks you for this indulgence. As you may know, I have been un-well. There is suspicion that the sickness may have infected someone from your ranks. The mystics ask permission to see the energy of those that attend you."

It was not strictly the truth, but Ielle knew it would not do to openly accuse the house of Obin of a misdeed. If there should be no problem found among them, it would cause ill-will between the two houses.

"As you wish, Kyr," Obin replied, satisfied with the explanation for now. He settled onto furs and had his second next to him. He waved to his men and girls to take up position on the wall opposite Kyr's men. The mystics approached him and repeat-ed the process. Obin's crystal glowed blue and green, vibrant and healthy. There was a similar response from his second and the rest of his men.

The mystics stood before Obin's girls, starting with Bata. When she brought the rocks together, there was a yellow cast. The other girls showed blues and greens. Again the mystics returned to the brazier and added more drops of liquids, consulting the steam.

"Hausa, there is a problem with this one." They pointed to Bata who became pale at the accusation. Before anyone could react, the mystic went on. "But Hausa, there is something else, someone else within your walls. This one hides something, we are sure, but is not enough to account for what we feel."

"By the gods," Obin bellowed. "What is this, Bata?"

Kyr held up a hand. "One moment please, Obin. There is more here first if you don't mind." Obin settled back. "Bylar, Makir, who else is not here? Is there someone hiding within my walls?" Bylar and Makir looked confused, talking quietly with Kyr a moment. Kaiu shifted, then gently eased herself from Ielle's side, slipping to Kyr's feet. Ielle struggled to hold herself upright without her support.

"Kyr, might I speak?"

He looked softy at his Ummi even though she interrupted his business. "Yes, my Ummi."

Kyr, there is one who is not here. Mayia is still in the cellar is she not?"

Bylar sprang up and shot out of the hall. "Thank you, Ummi, that was wise. I had forgotten her presence is still within my walls. Perhaps we shall get to the bottom of things now." Kyr patted her hand gently and stroked her cheek.

"Obin, my apologies for all this. I do not yet know what to make of this news but we shall see when this girl arrives if there is a story that includes your property."

Bylar entered dragging Mayia along. He dumped her into a pile at the feet of the mystics. Ielle sucked in her breath at her appearance. Her hair was tangled and filthy, her skin covered with bruises and welts. Bylar's chain hung loosely from her hips. There were dried fluids on her, her gaze was dulled. It was painful to look at and even more painful to think this could be her own fate soon too.

The mystic gave her the crystals and the seed, bidding her to bring them together. For the first time Ielle could remember, Mayia complied with an instruction immediately, moving them until they touched. The bottom of the crystals was so dark it looked black. Above it was the same yellow that Bata's crystal showed and beyond that was a brilliant red. The mystic quickly took a step back when he saw the display. Bylar removed the crystals from her hands and handed them back.

"Hausa, this one hides something as well, and her heart is black. She carries hatred and greed. You should question her further, and that other too."

CHAPTER TWENTY
~ KYR ~

"Mayia, on your feet." Bylar hauled her up at Kyr's words. "What is it that the mystic speaks of? I know you know what it is. Speak."

"Hausa, I, I do not know." Her voice was soft and ragged.

"She lies still. I do not need a mystic to see that."

"Hausa," the mystic said. "If I do not overstep, I have something that may help. It is a potion that encourages truth telling. It is most uncomfortable, she would have a terrible itching and burning in her core, but she would be compelled to tell the truth in all things. We do not use it often. It will ruin her permanently."

"Excellent idea. I do not care what pains she suffers. Administer it." He heard Ielle gasp but he could not look at her right now. He did not know yet what he might hear and what part Ielle might have in it, he could not know if she would not be next. He nodded to Ummi and she returned to Ielle's side. The mystic set to work mixing ingredients.

"And while we wait for it to take effect, Obin, do you mind if I should question your girl?" Obin waved his hand in agreement.

"Bata, to me here. Naku." She rose and made her way to Kyr, hesitating over the order and looking to Obin. "Obin, I hope you do not think me too forward, but I find that when a girl has something to hide, her nakedness helps bring that to the light."

"Excellent point, Kyr. Naku, Bata. And you will answer to Kyr of Janos as though he was your master. Do not embarrass my house, girl." She had gone pale again, slipping off her robes and letting them puddle on the ground. She was naked except for Obin's chain about her waist. Kyr could see by the way she held herself that she was used to getting what she wanted from men. That would not work with him.

"Tell me, Bata, what is it that you hide?"

"Nothing, Master."

"See, Obin, her skin flushes on her chest. That is a sign that she lies." Obin nodded, noting it as true.

"Bata, do you see Mayia?"

"Yes, Master."

"I did that to her. Do you really mean to make me take similar steps with you?" He watched her face as she glanced again to Mayia, still held by Bylar, standing before them all in her wretched state. "Do not think that Obin would save you. He has said you are to answer to me as your master. I would take any steps I like. I could have the mystic administer the same potion to you."

"I ask again, Bata." He leaned forward and spit each word at her. "What is it that you hide?"

"Only about the potion, Master." She ducked her head, her skin flushed from head to chest in embarrassment.

"What potion, Bata?" He watched as she shot another look at Mayia, weighing her options. Good, weigh them well, girl. Bylar's hand was digging tightly into Mayia's arm to keep her on her feet. Her skin was deathly pale, making her bruises and welts stand out even further. The mystic was forcing a small amount of liquid between her lips. Bata gulped at the reality of what could happen then words began to tumble from her freely.

"The potion to make you refuse your girl, Master."

"What?" Obin thundered, rising to his feet and storming over to her. She cowered, sinking quickly to her knees before him, pressing her lips to his feet. "Speak, Bata, now. All of it." He pulled her back up and turned her towards Kyr, not allowing her to hide anything.

"I had a potion that was to make you lose interest in your girl. It was just an entertainment, to punish your girl. She was so well used. We could all see it. Our jealousy got the better of us. It would be amusing to see her wanting for a week or two. It was foolish, a silly girl's game, Master."

Stupid kafai. Another waste of a girl. Kyr leaned forward again. "How did you deliver this potion, Bata?"

"I soaked some pakoul berries in it, Master. I knew Ielle would select them for your meal." Out of the corner of his eye he caught a flinch from Ielle. Could it be she did not know? He didn't dare to hope yet. There was so much more to come.

"And where did this potion come from, Bata?" She looked down and shuffled her feet, not wanting to answer. Obin grabbed a handful of her hair and tipped her head back.

"From Mayia, Master," she said quietly. Mayia was now dancing from foot to foot, squirming and trying to rub her thighs together. Good. It was working on her. Bylar lashed her hands behind her back so that she could not rub herself. Excellent. He hauled her over to the wall and chained her legs apart. Now she could not rub her thighs together either. Perfect.

"Ah, and how did I know you had your hand in this too, Mayia?" He turned to Makir and sent him on an errand. The evidence would clear things up once and for all.

"Bata," Kyr went on, "How did you know Ielle would select the berries for me?"

Mayia said so, Master." Mayia was frantically rubbing her rear against the wall but could not manage to find relief that way.

Makir returned to the room with something in his hand. "Show it to her, Makir." He held the vial before Bata. "Is this the potion?"

She blanched and looked as though she might faint. "Yes, Master."

"Obin, your girl has been used by one of the house of Kyr of Janos. My apologies to you. She was told this potion was something other than what it is. Bad enough yes, but it seems she did not know that it was in truth a poison. She was a pawn in a plot to remove me as Hausa." The stupid kafai did faint. Good. It was the most useful she'd been in her existence. He was confident she did not know the true intent of what she did. It was Mayia that moved her hand. One of Obin's guards started towards her but Obin held up his hand and left the girl slumped where she landed.

"And you, Mayia, you would try to bring down the house of Kyr of Janos, eh? To what end, girl?"

She was squirming and whimpering, desperately trying to alleviate the burning between her thighs. "Yes, Master, yes. Bylar should be Hausa, then I would be high woman of the house. No other girl would serve over me. No other girl would have the high favor then."

Kyr blew out his breath. Yes, this all made sense. The stupid, stupid girl. Jealousy and greed, sneakiness. The ways of women of no character. Not the way of his Ielle.

"And how did you get the vial among Ielle's things, Mayia?"

"Once the searches started, I feared having it, so I sewed it into some furs and left it with the chamber maid's things. She brought it into your chamber without even knowing. Please, please, Master, I cannot stand this burning, please." She was wailing and keening, but he paid it no mind.

"And where did you get such a potion, Mayia?"

"From a vendor of healing oils, Master. I told him I wished to get rid of some vermin and he provided it to me in exchange for some favors. Master, please, I would do anything to make this stop."

"Return her to the cellar, Bylar. She can continue her punishment there until we have time to take her for the discard. Perhaps if she can service enough men that will relieve her current discomfort in a week or two. If not, I imagine it will increase her desire to work hard at the rentals, if there's anything left of her by then. Obin, thank you for your indulgence. Again, my apologies for how your property was brought into our little drama."

"It is I that apologize, Kyr. I knew she was flighty and stupid, but she entertains in the furs. I had no idea she was so useless. I shall deal with her immediately, you can be sure."

"It is no matter, Obin. When I have fully recovered, we shall share a banquet and enjoy the dances and service of pleasing girls. Now, however, I apologize again, but I must return to my chamber. Our girls will be at your service, Makir shall lead the hall tonight for you. No pakoul berries tonight though, eh?"

Obin laughed with him. "Of course, of course. We shall be gone in the morning and not impose on your hospitality further. I thank you for bringing this to my attention." Obin clapped his hands and his men and girls filed out. Bata was dragged out by one of his guards. Kyr dismissed his men and girls as well. There was one more thing to take care of.

"Remove her binding." Tears were flowing freely. Both Ummi and Ielle sobbed. The guard quickly unleashed Ielle and helped her up gently. Kyr leaned heavily on Makir and the party made their way to Kyr's chamber.

Kyr was settled into his furs and Ielle was placed carefully beside him. Ah, Ielle. His beautiful Ielle. He pulled her to his side, her soft naked skin along his own, taking care not to press on her damaged side. He rested her head against his chest, stroking his fingers through her hair. Ummi bustled around them, calling out orders to bring things from her chamber for Ielle's care, sending Ama off for additional items for Kyr. Makir stood close and tried to help, all of them only succeeding in getting in each other's way.

"Ielle-kyr, my girl," he said quietly into her ear. "It is well these people are here because I think it might kill us both if I were to take you as I wish right now." She smiled at him and snuggled closer against him, tracing her fingers over his chest.

"Kyr, I am so happy now, I can hardly speak. First I feared you would die. Then I feared I should never see you again." He dropped a kiss on the top of her head. His poor Ielle. She had borne more pain than even he had, first fearing for his life, then being imprisoned and abused, unjustly accused, threatened with a terrible fate and all the while she only cared for his well being. She was strong, his Ielle. She fought to survive and to be with him. It was a tremendous gift to have her utmost devotion. He was fortunate to have wise, strong women around him.

"Ummi!" He called her to his side. "Ummi, all is well now. Ielle-kyr is here, we rest. Ama serves us,

Makir and Bylar assist. Rest now, Ummi. Or must I send you to share the cellar with Mayia to make you listen?" He grinned at her and she laughed.

"The poor girl wouldn't be able to stand it. I may be an old woman, but I know that I am much more pleasing, especially in the furs!" Kyr blushed, hearing his Ummi speak so. Yes, she would leave Mayia in the dust.

"But so that you're not tempted to try it out, I will go and rest. I will check on you two tomorrow. And you are both to rest."

"Yes, Ummi. Thank you for your wisdom. We are both in your debt."

"Kaiu, thank you," Ielle said. "Please, I do not know how I can ever repay you."

"You will start by calling me Ummi as Kyr does, Ielle. You are a daughter to me. I would be honored if you should address me such."

"Oh, Ummi! Of course! It would be my honor," Ielle said, wiping new tears from her eyes. They embraced, reaching over Kyr to do so, both of them crying happy tears. Kyr laughed at the emotions, feeling them himself but showing more control.

"All right, all right, enough of this blubbering you two. Off to rest, Ummi. Ielle and I need our sleep now."

CHAPTER TWENTY-ONE
~ IELLE ~

She woke in Kyr's arms, his heart beating under her head. All was right with her world. He stirred a moment later, stroking his hands over her back.

"Good dawn to you, Ielle-kyr." He pressed his lips into her hair. "I have missed you." He trailed his fingers over her face, a sadness in his eyes.

"Good dawn to you, Kyr of Janos. And I have missed you also." She looked up at him and rested her hand over his as he traced her face.

"You are a good girl, Ielle-kyr. I am sorry for the pain you've had, especially that which I created." He stroked the cheek he had slapped. She brought his hand to her mouth and kissed it softly.

"It is all done now, Kyr. It could have been

much, much worse. We are well now, release it. Relax, accept, submit. Find harmony. I have done so."

"You're a wise girl, Ielle-kyr." She trailed fingers across his chest then sucked his nipple into her mouth, teasing it with her tongue.

"Be careful, Ielle-kyr. I do not think either of us is up to a passionate encounter right now. Do not ignite the flame, my girl." He grinned at her and she smiled back.

"Yes, it would be a shame to survive the poison and the ribs only to die with you slotted in me, thrusting and pumping, sucking you dry, shaking my breasts in your face..." She grinned back at him. He slapped his hand on her rear.

"You are a wanton girl, Ielle-kyr."

"You have made me so, Kyr of Janos."

~

The healer came later that morning, examining them both and pronouncing them fit enough for the baths. Kyr brought her to his pool and she gently eased into the warm bubbling water. Heavenly. The water wrapped around her, massaging her sore spots. Kyr sighed when he sank down in the water beside her. She snuggled into him, unable to stop touching him.

"Kyr, what will happen to Mayia?"

"That kuckai will be discarded and sent to the rentals. The Oblate will impose a punishment first. You know this, do you not?" He played with her hair, running it through his fingers.

"Yes, I know that, and she does deserve it, she brought it on herself. I meant the truth potion."

Kyr laughed heartily. "Well, my girl, first I must ask why you care? Do you hold compassion for such a creature?"

"Not compassion exactly." It was hard to explain how she felt. "Curiosity perhaps. Pity."

"Do you seek revenge?"

"No, I have no interest in revenge, truly. There is nothing I could do that would harm her as she harmed me. She does not care for anyone as I care for you, so there would be nothing that could touch her the same way."

"Very true."

"It is just that there are expectations in our life. She knew what might befall her if she took such an action, so it is right and due that she now reaps it. The truth potion seems to be something beyond what is promised. Not entirely undeserved, but still somewhat more than anyone would foresee."

"You are a good girl, Ielle-kyr. Do not trouble yourself over it. Likely it has already worn off. There really is no truth potion."

"What?" She groaned, having moved a bit too

quickly when she heard his words. He settled her back against him, soothing over her back.

"I arranged it with the mystics before we began. I did not know it would be Mayia that we would use it on, but I thought maybe it would be a way to bring the truth to light. It causes fierce itching and burning but it wears off in a few hours. That is all it does. It was her own guilt and the idea that it would bring the truth that made her speak it. Besides, if there were a truth potion, no matter what the effects, do you not think you would hear of its use?"

"Yes, I suppose I would have. It is good then, Kyr." She rubbed her cheek on his chest. "Kyr..."

"My but you're full of questions today are you not?" He smiled at her.

She smiled back. "Yes, so it seems. Is Bylar well?"

Kyr sighed. "He carries wounds as we do, Iellekyr. But like us, I believe he will recover in time."

They spent much time soaking in the baths over the next few days. Ummi hovered over them, ensuring that they eat well. On the third day the healer allowed them to start taking walks around the house. Though neither was moving at full force, they leaned on each other and made laps through the halls. Kyr began seeing his advisors again and Ielle returned to managing the household.

The only thing that was still not right was Bylar. He stayed away from Ielle and Kyr, attending only

when required, preferring to take a post in the hallway on the other side of Kyr's door rather than be in
the room if he could. It saddened Ielle's heart to have
him so.

~

The day arrived for the discard. Ielle still wore the
binding and the plaster but she was much improved.
She no longer struggled to breathe and only had
twinges of pain when she moved too quickly.

"You will attend with us, Ielle-kyr. You and
Ummi are the ones she has most wronged. It is right
that you witness, and right that she see you do it."

He had her adorned in an even more intricate
weaving of blue ropes than she wore before. The
chamber maids glued an incredible sparkling blue
gemstone into her navel. Rouge was applied to nipples and lips, colored powders to her face and eye-
lids. True she still wore the binding for her ribs, but
the ropes made her feel beautiful for Kyr. She hoped
she would represent him well.

Dawn was just breaking when he placed her
gently on the mareshi, sitting her sideways. He took
his spot behind her, holding her closely against him
to guard her from the jostling of the beast. Ummi was
settled carefully with Makir. Bylar dragged Mayia to
his mount, tossing her over it harshly and strapping

her down. It was the same position Ielle had ridden in all that time ago, but worse. She was over the rump of the animal and tightly bound at hands and feet as well as across the middle. It would be much more painful for Mayia than it had been for her. Mayia was thin now too. Where she used to be adorned in red robes, now she was adorned in welts and bruises. It did not seem she had been washed since she was sent to the cellar. And her true punishment was yet to come.

Ielle shuddered, remembering how close she came to a similar fate. Kyr tightened his hold on her and kissed at her neck. It seemed that possibility touched him too.

They were off! The mareshi lurched forward but she was hardly bounced at all this time, Kyr was taking great care with her. They rode from dawn to just before the noon, stopping at a tavern. Ielle blushed remembering her last visit to such a place, but she did not think Kyr would repeat it with Ummi there as well.

Mayia was left bound to the mareshi. There would be no relief for her even while they supped. Ielle served the men, moving slower than usual still but so happy to be able to perform for them again. She prepared the plate and moved it softly over her skin from thighs to heart, feeling so much she was afraid she might cry. She brought it to her lips, kissing it for him, bowing her head.

"Your meal is prepared and humbly served. May it serve you well and your girl be forever pleasing." She waited for him to take the plate, drawing air into her lungs, feeling almost like the first time she served him. It was good to be able to do this again. He slipped it from her hands, caressing them when he did it. She looked up and he locked eyes with her, reminding her of all the times she had ever served and all the ways she had done so. He nodded for her to continue and she presented plates to Makir and Bylar. Bylar was still reluctant to look at her, taking the plate from her with a grunt. Perhaps when the discard was complete he would begin to heal too.

Kyr pulled her into his lap and fed her, but unlike the last time, he did not fondle her. Ummi was there so she was pleased he did not. She would be utterly mortified if he did, but at the same time, she missed his touch. She hoped she would soon be ready for his use again.

When they came back outside it was clear that Mayia had not been neglected. There were bright sharp handprints across her naked ass. Anything was fair if one was left by oneself in front of a tavern, especially in such a condition.

It was shortly after that they reached the dais where the discard would be conducted. This was not the same place or the same Oblate that had conducted the ceremony with Ielle and Kyr. They were still within the outer reaches of Janos so it would not be the location where Bylar and Mayia had their ceremony either.

Ielle and Ummi were carefully handed down from the mareshi. Mayia was unbound and then shoved off the mareshi, landing hard in a heap on the ground. She whimpered, but did not carry on as she might have done a short time ago. Perhaps even Mayia was capable of learning after all.

The Oblate was ready. Kyr and Bylar mounted the dais first, taking their positions standing before the Oblate. Ielle and Ummi followed, kneeling beside them. Makir threw Mayia over his shoulder and carried her to the feet of the Oblate, dumping her off with another hard landing. Makir untied her feet so that she could stand and dragged her upright, holding her so that she could not bolt. The journey had not improved her appearance. Tear stains streaked her face, her hair hung in strings where it was not clumped and matted. She moved stiffly, obviously in pain from the method of travel.

"Who owns this property?"

"Bylar of Janos."

"Who stands with the owner?"

"Kyr of Janos." The scribe wrote quickly on the tablet.

"By what name has the property been known?"

"Mayia-bylar of Janos."

And what is the charge?"

Ielle listened closely. It was enough to merely say a girl was not pleasing.

"She abused the property of the Hausa." Bylar's voice rang clear and steady. Murmurs ran through the crowd. The Oblate held up his hand for silence.

"She offered herself to men without knowledge or permission of her owner." Again the whispers in the crowd.

"She attempted to poison the Hausa." The crowd was loud now, jeering at Mayia. Ielle felt Ummi flinch next to her. The hostility was so strong, it was good to know it was not directed towards them, but still it was alarming. Even the Oblate seemed surprised to hear this charge, taking his own step back from the girl. He conferred a moment with the scribe.

"Does she confess to these crimes?"

"Yes, Oblate, she does. In front of the house of Kyr of Janos as well as many members of the house of Obin of Mashet."

Mayia raised her head. "Oblate, it is lies."

The crowd gasped nearly as one. It was shocking to think a girl would address the Oblate, even more so that she should make out her owner to be a liar, especially one who served so closely to a Hausa.

"What is it that you say, girl?" The Oblate turned to her, his hand raised to still the crowd.

"He forced the confession from me, with trickery and deceit. Him! The Hausa, Kyr of Janos." She pointed her finger at Kyr and glared at him. "He lies about me to keep his property from finding out that he visits me daily. He is afraid she will refuse to serve him if she knows the truth. He is afraid his brother Bylar will be annoyed he uses me without his leave."

Ielle felt her stomach drop. Kyr's shoulders tightened. She could feel his anger and how he worked to restrain himself. Bylar looked as though he took a blow to his midsection. The crowd was wild with whispers and jeers.

The Oblate turned to Kyr. "How do you answer this charge?"

"It is beyond absurd, Oblate. As the Hausa I may take her as I like, leave or no, with no care for anything except politeness among men. As it is, she has been offered to me many times and has never once served me."

He turned to Bylar. "Forgive the bluntness, my brother, but I have never found her to be pleasing enough to bother with. Whatever charms she possesses have always escaped me, totally overtaken by her petulance."

Bylar nodded acknowledging his words. His shoulders seemed further weighted with this new burden.

"It is Ielle! She masters him in secret! She lies to drive me away. She is jealous that I am more pleasing to her owner!" Mayia was screaming, frantic, her face ugly with rage, she dropped to the floor shrieking.

"Enough." Bylar straightened and spoke firmly. "Oblate, as her owner, I stand not only with my brother Kyr, but also with what I have seen with my own eyes. There is nothing to her words. Clearly I cannot say how she has been spending her days, but I know how Kyr spends his. As you have just heard, he would never speak anything but the truth to me no matter if I wanted to hear. She merely seeks to cause trouble and spread dissent within his walls to the end."

The Oblate nodded. He had a quiet word with the scribe. There was a long discussion between them.

"We proceed with the discard. I find the words of Mayia-bylar to be false."

"Kuckai, Ielle! Tispe!"

The crowd was shocked into a deadly silence. Ielle felt her heart in her throat. Even men did not speak such words where an Oblate might hear. They were direct representatives of the gods. It was an extreme sacrilege.

Bylar stepped forward, calmly wrapping his hand in her hair and using it to pull her to her feet while she howled. He stared at her. Ielle had never known his eyes to look so cold, as though any lingering emotion for her was wiped clean by her actions.

211

Without warning he slapped her soundly across the face then dropped her back to the ground.

"My sincere apologies to you and the gods. It seems that I am even more remiss in exercising control over my property than I knew. There is no one she will not attempt to defile."

The Oblate nodded accepting his apology. "The punishment is decided. She will be impaled front and rear in the square for a period of one full moon. She will then be sold to a rental in a land at least three sectors removed from Janos."

Mayia let out an unholy keen. The scribe came to her and used a tool to snap the chain at her waist. The chain popped loudly when it was severed. Ielle closed her eyes and took a breath. Even the lust of the crowd was a bit taken aback. Being displayed in the square was severe, being impaled on a hard, fat phallus, and in both holes was, extreme. Rarely were public punishments made for more than a day or two. This would be an entire moon. And it would start tomorrow on the dawn so that she might have nearly a day to contemplate what was to come. Still, it was no less than she deserved. Mayia had chosen her path poorly and showed her true colors to the end.

CHAPTER TWENTY-TWO
~ KYR ~

Kyr felt lighter once the sentence was announced. Ummi and Ielle were clearly shaken, but it was good to have it done. It was hard to read Bylar. He knew him. He would have relief and regret both on many levels. It would take some time.

They left immediately after the record was signed. There was no reason to linger here, no reason to wallow in the girl's fate. The Oblate agreed to accept her sale money as payment for himself and the scribe, so there would be no reason for Bylar to return at the end of the moon to conduct the sale. They could wash their hands, it was done.

He stroked his hand along Ielle's thigh, so happy to have her resting against him. It was like their first trip on the mareshi, she leaned on him and drifted into slumber, trusting him to keep her safe. She was still recovering, the trip was taxing to her, physically and emotionally. Still, he was sure it was good for her to be there and see things through.

He gently woke Ielle as they crossed into his gates. He slipped her down from the mareshi, taking the time to slide his hands over the intricate ropes. He looked deeply into her eyes, drowning in her devotion to him. A low growl rose from him when he brought his mouth down over hers, taking her, claiming her, reminding her she was owned. She melted into him, giving him everything. He pulled back and tried to catch his breath. It had been so long, it was hard to keep control. She was still injured, he must be careful with her.

The mareshi moved and he was brought back, realizing they were still standing in the courtyard surrounded by other people. He sighed. This was not the place and probably not yet the time. They would have a quiet meal in his chambers tonight. Soon they would all be back to normal.

He relaxed naked in his furs, holding her against him, playing with the blue ropes that bound her skin. Ielle shifted and brought her lips to his nipple, sucking it and teasing it with her tongue. He groaned and tried to gently nudge her off but she pushed back, insisting.

"Please, Kyr. I need your touch." Her fingers were dancing on his skin.

"I don't want to hurt you, Ielle-kyr." By the gods how he wanted her.

"I'm tougher than I look." She rubbed a thigh over his leg.

"Yes, I know you are." She held up so well, for him.

She captured his hand in hers bringing it to her breast, resting it over the nipple. "Please, Kyr. Let me serve you, please."

He could not keep himself from kneading the soft flesh under his fingers. She leaned into his touch, begging for more. She was so beautiful. More so with the blue rope making diamonds over her skin. He slipped a finger under the part that bisected her crotch, wiggling it, knowing it would bring the knot in close contact with her sex. She gasped and shifted her hips, pumping into the feeling.

"By the gods, Ielle-kyr. You torment me!"

She smiled and moved off him, getting onto her hands and knees and backing her rear end up to him. "My side is still somewhat sore, yes. But this end works just fine, see?" She wiggled her hips and spread her legs apart, giving him a peek at her tender lips.

"Does it now?" He slapped his hands down on her rear, watching the skin redden between the blue rope frame, grinning at her squeak. He stroked a finger

215

along the twin cords that ran over her crotch, sliding between them and entering her. She gasped and squirmed under his touch. He added a second finger and she moaned, soft, low noises coming from her. He moved to his knees, still working his fingers in her, his other hand one tracing the pattern across her back. He leaned over her, not resting his weight on her, but reaching under to capture a nipple, pinching and tugging at it.

"Kyr, Kyr... I am your property, please, use me well." Her voice was raspy and quiet, pleading and needy.

He took his fingers from her, wiping them on her rear. He gave a pinch high to her inner thigh, hearing her quick intake, soothing after with a stroke of his finger along her cleft. The sharp and the soft. Bringing her close, then backing off. Making her feel more, be more. He pinched hard on her nipple giving it a twist until she whimpered. He leaned over her and licked his tongue across the back of her neck. She would not know what was next or where it might land. His lips on the small of her back, his sharp tug on the rope between her legs, sliding his chain through his fingers and over her skin. It was working in concert on her, centering all her awareness on her body and how it served him.

He was so hard and ready. He had waited so long. He settled his hands against her hips, holding her steady, then slotted his hard cock between the strands. He let his breath out, holding still a moment, giving them both time to get used to the sensation. She was panting, waiting for him to go on. She pulsed her muscles against him, encouraging him to do more, teasing him in her woman's way.

He clenched his fingers hard into her hips. His fingers dimpled the skin and she moaned anew. He heard her, quiet and soft, saying his name. She was totally his. He pulled back slowly, nearly out, then slid in again. She dropped to her elbows, raising her ass even higher for him. Again, he made the slow move back and forth, knowing it was not enough for her, not enough for him. By the gods, he could not stand it. He held her hips tightly, hoping not to jostle her too much and then thrusting, solid and sure, deeply, fully. Filling her, over and over, hitting inside her. Her gasps and moans drove him, his balls slapped against her, the knot of the rope rubbed her. She released, screaming for him, totally his in every way, pulling his release from him. Totally his.

He laid back and moved to pull her onto his chest to rest, but she pulled back, settling between his legs instead, using her mouth to clean their fluids from him. She peeked at him, licking her tongue from the base to the tip, flirting with him, teasing. She swallowed him fully into her mouth, stroking her lips up and down, sucking, dancing her tongue on him.

ANDRÉ SANTHOMAS

"You are a wanton girl, Ielle-kyr."

She slipped off him and moved up to cuddle on his chest. "You have made me so, Kyr of Janos."

~

It was a few days later when Bylar arrived at the door to his chambers.

"My Hausa, may I speak with you?"

"Why so formal, Bylar? You are my dear friend and brother, my confidant and second. You may always speak with me, in my chambers, the pools, the halls, wherever we are. There has never been a need for permission." Bylar fidgeted. Kyr could not recall ever seeing him thus. Kyr waved to him to enter and join him.

Ielle shifted, kneeling by his side, resting her head on his knee. She looked to him, questioning if she should stay or go.

"Kyr, if it should please you, I would like her to stay," Bylar said, crossing the room and standing before him. He was breathing quickly, his skin was flushed, sweat broke out on his brow.

"Of course, Bylar." He stroked his fingers through Ielle's hair and eyed him with concern. "Please, sit and relax. Is there some service you would enjoy? Should you like me to call a house girl for you?"

"No, no, Kyr, not necessary." Bylar sat down heavily. He plucked at a thread on his pants.

"Kyr..." He stopped and took another deep breath.

"By the gods, man, what is it?"

"I have brought pain to you, to your property, to your household. So many ways I have wronged you..." He shook his head. "I did not protect you, I did not protect your property. I brought that kuckai inside your walls and kept her here despite all good sense. I did not fulfill my role as your friend, your brother, your protector. I cannot stay within your walls, Kyr. With your permission, I must take my leave."

"Bylar-"

"No, Kyr, please, let me finish." Kyr raised an eyebrow at the interruption but allowed him to go on. "I have been over these words a thousand times, they must be said now." He looked towards Ielle. "I have been the cause of great wrongs to you all. Please know that I would never do so with any intention. But in life, it is not enough to mean well. One must do well and I have not. As my last duty as your protector, Kyr, I must protect you from such a fool as myself."

Kyr laughed out loud. It felt good to laugh deeply. He had not done so since he had word of a traitor in his midst. Ielle caressed his thigh thoughtfully, watching the conversation flowing back and forth between them. Bylar was looking at him like he lost his mind. "Bylar, I would gladly take an army of fools such as yourself over learned men or wizened thinkers. How can you think yourself a fool?"

Bylar started to answer, but this time Kyr cut him off with a raised hand. "No, Bylar. I will grant that you chose poorly for your property." He shrugged. "Such is life. You will choose better next time. But as soon as there was danger to your Hausa, your brother and your friend, you were there. My closest ally. Protecting me and my household."

"But Kyr, I did not protect you or your household."

"Ridiculous, Bylar, of course you did. Did you not search every nook within my walls until you found the potion? Did you not contain the one you thought was the source of the harm? Did you not secure my room and keep out those that might harm me further in my condition? Did you not bring the healer? Did you not stay by side, run my household and serve my interests?"

"But none of that would have been needed if I had not unwittingly set the events into motion in the first place. It is not enough to clean up the mess when you are the one who created it foolishly."

"Is it not enough? Do you think you are of the gods, Bylar that you will never err? Do you put yourself above the rest of us?"

"Of course not! But I have failed in my duty."

Again, the shrug from Kyr. "Not as I see it and I am still the Hausa, am I not? Fail again in the same way, I'll send you to the stable boys for their entertainment." He grinned.

"Otherwise, I need you by my side, Bylar." He smiled at his friend and clapped him on the shoulder. Ielle caught his attention.

"Master, may I speak please?" He smiled down at his property and nodded. She made her way to Bylar's feet, kneeling before him with her thighs respectfully closed, head bowed.

"I wish to thank you, Bylar." She looked up at him with tears in her eyes. "You worked to save the life of my master and I will be forever indebted to you."

"You do not harbor ill will towards me, Ielle?"

"How could I, Bylar? You protected him from all threats, no matter how painful that was for you."

"Return to your master, Ielle." His voice was rough and it was clear he was touched by her words.

"Then we shall have no more talk of you leaving, Bylar. And when you are ready, we will find you some pleasing property."

"I wonder if I should ever find such a thing, but perhaps."

"Come now, we shall put all this behind us. I owe that fool Obin a merriment. We will schedule something, invite all our allies. A big event to show all that the house of Kyr of Janos still stands."

~THE END~

About the Author

André first met her husband when she threw herself
at his feet in an on-line paga den.
Now she writes stories about gloriously submissive
females at the feet of
delightfully dominant men.

You can follow her at andresanthomas.blogspot.com
or write her at andresanthomas@gmail.com.

Look for the Realm of Janos Series
IELLE
OVIA
EANNA
MAYIA

And for something fun, try
INSIDE THE REALM OF JANOS
TV SERIES FANTASY

Also by André SanThomas

SENSUAL SUBMISSION: DRIVEN
SENSUAL SUBMISSION: PURSUIT

OVIA

A REALM OF JANOS NOVEL

BY

ANDRÉ SANTHOMAS

CHAPTER ONE ~ BYLAR

Makir thrust steady and sure into the girl spread out on the altar. Bylar held the girl's hands tightly behind her back, feeling her clench and tense. The thrusting pushed the slight girl against his broad chest, but it was no problem for him to hold her up to watch Makir work. The ceremony required that she see the one who would own and possess her. It was Bylar's charge to ensure it would happen.

She was shaking and whimpering, clenching his hands tightly, stronger than he would have expected from such a tiny girl. She was panting, then moaning, then suddenly arching her back and letting loose with a long slow groan that sounded like something between pain and pleasure. Makir's release came immediately after, his eyes closing, his

229

own grunt spilling from him, holding himself deeply inside her for a moment while he filled her. Yes, he was spent.

Bylar remembered his own ceremony with Mayia. It was heavenly to take her, but he deceived himself by thinking he ever really owned her. She allowed him to pretend he did. He was careless enough to think he did, but when it all went ever so badly, he realized he had only been fooling himself all along. He shook the ugly old thoughts from his head and focused on his friend Makir. Young Makir, deciding he was ready to petition for his own property. Makir had matured after Kyr nearly died, stepping up in Bylar's absence and taking charge of things in the midst of a dire time. He had a new found confidence that was impressive but not cocky. So much so that he rejected the first girl the Council offered him. He did not reject this one though, he had just taken her soundly before one and all.

Bylar laid the girl down on the altar gently, then Makir took her hands and pulled her to sit up and wait for the Oblate to approve the joining. The Oblate conferred with the scribe and reviewed the cloth. The Oblate held the cloth aloft and announced, "The contract is fulfilled." The crowd cheered and applauded, Kyr clapped Makir on the back. "Let this female forever be known as Norea-makir of Janos, property of the first order."

Makir was beaming. Hopefully the girl would continue to make him this happy and not turn into a harping scheming shrew. Once again Bylar pushed the black images from his mind. Logic told him there were many happy joinings, Ielle and Kyr were a fine example, but even after so many moons it was hard to get past the betrayal and pain that Mayia had wrought. The chain was placed on her slim hips, Makir's crest dangling from it to show who her owner was. It would remain on her forever, unless there should be the ugliness of a discard. The snap when his own chain was cut from Mayia's waist still echoed in his head.

Bylar bound the girl's hands behind her while Makir finished with the Oblate.

"How would you have her ride, Makir?" Bylar waited while Makir thought and considered. He could feel the girl tremble waiting to hear the answer.

"Seat her in front of me, legs astride, my friend." It was a good choice. Firm, commanding, she would know her place. Makir was setting a good tone. Much better than the one he had apparently set with his own girl. Bylar hefted her up, barely feeling her weight in his arms as he arranged her legs wide open over the broad back of the mareshi. She would be naked for the trip, no cloak or shift to make her think Makir would go soft. Her hands were behind her, so she would learn quickly to lean into Makir, let him protect and guide her. It was good. Those things he had not thought important for himself, Makir had learned by his poor example. At least there was something to come from it all.

He sighed as he took his own seat on the mareshi. Truth be told, he did miss having his own property. There were always house girls willing to serve in any way he desired. Some of them were especially enchanting and enticing in the furs, but there was something wonderful about owning property, knowing you had claimed her, building her devotion to you beyond what her duty required. It was a special thing and he felt its loss. He probably never really experienced it with Mayia, but he still felt grief at the loss of what he thought he had.

Kyr was after him to petition for a new girl. Perhaps it was time. There was the saying about how a new nail driven in straight, true and strong would push out an old one no matter how bent it might be. A new piece of property might push out the demons that lingered from the old one. It was hard to know what to do. Perhaps the gods would give him a sign. He would look for one in the next few days and know how he should proceed.

They spent the night camping in the woods, Bylar and Kyr taking their things to the other side of the mareshi to give some semblance of privacy to

Makir. They talked quietly, each lost in thoughts of the night when it was their turn with their new property. They heard grunts and groans and a few sharp smacks. Bylar teased Kyr about the loud whimpers and screams that still rang out from Kyr's chamber when he used Ielle.

He slept restlessly. Usually he enjoyed sleeping out of doors, looking up at the heavens. This night he was plagued with jumbled visions of Mayia and her treachery, the near loss of Kyr, the near loss of Ielle, the toll it took on them all. He tossed and turned and several times woke in a sweat, uneasy and anxious, ready to protect Kyr from some unseen predator before realizing there was none. The demon that he brought inside Kyr's walls was long gone.

He rose at the dawn and had a quick splash in the crystal orange waters of the nearby stream to clear his head. His most important job was protection for Kyr. He could not get slack from fatigue or errant thoughts. He had done enough to harm Kyr. He swore he would never let him down again. Norea was so light he practically tossed her back onto the mareshi in the same position as the day before. She was glowing, her eyes bright, snuggling into Makir like she had been doing it for years. It did not seem to concern her that she was naked, her legs spread wide open, her hands bound, as long as she had Makir's arms around her guiding the mareshi reins.

When they crossed the stone bridge over the Janosa waterway, he relaxed a bit. It was always good to be back in Janos. He could take the more relaxed riding position alongside Kyr instead of in front of him. If only he could let his racing mind relax in the same way. He thought he had let so much of it go over the last few moons. On the surface he laughed and joked. Makir's ceremony brought it all to the forefront again.

Throughout the ride he saw nothing but pairs of animals. When they stopped to water the mareshi a bird's nest caught his eye. The fledglings chirped from their safe perch in the nest. Two birds swooped and played overhead, then the proud male bird broke away. The male landed on the branch nearby watching over the fledgling birds, delicate and fragile. The mother returned with food for her babies. When they were fed, the mother bird tucked herself against the male bird, nestled under his wing.

Was this his sign? Did the gods want him to try again? Why would they let him fail the first time? Perhaps there were lessons to learn. He would not be so slack next time, of that he was sure. Was it enough? There was no way to know. It was also said that if one did not gamble one could not lose. He had already lost so much once. Was he strong enough to gamble again?

They made their way along the road, passing the forest that lined the Janosa waterway. A majestic buck darted out, followed a moment later by his mate. They sprang across the path, ducking back into the woods. The buck led, the doe followed. He sighed. He could not deny it. Clearly, it was meant to be. He would try again. Kyr would stand with him. Could he choose well this time? Only the gods would know.